Beyond the Covenant
And Other Stories

To Judy –

James F. Gaines

A wonderful writer, editor, and friend

Jim Gaines

James F. Gaines
FREDERICKSBURG, VIRGINIA

Copyright © 2016 by James F. Gaines.

All rights reserved. No part of this publication may be reproduced, distributed or transmitted in any form or by any means, including photocopying, recording, or other electronic or mechanical methods, without the prior written permission of the publisher, except in the case of brief quotations embodied in critical reviews and certain other noncommercial uses permitted by copyright law. For permission requests, write to the publisher, addressed "Attention: Permissions Coordinator," at the address below.

James F. Gaines
17 North Pointe Dr.
Fredericksburg, Virginia 22405
www.jmrgaines.com

Publisher's Note: This is a work of fiction. Names, characters, places, and incidents are a product of the author's imagination. Locales and public names are sometimes used for atmospheric purposes. Any resemblance to actual people, living or dead, or to businesses, companies, events, institutions, or locales is completely coincidental.

Book Layout & Design ©2013 - BookDesignTemplates.com

Ordering Information:
Quantity sales. Special discounts are available on quantity purchases by corporations, associations, and others. For details, contact the "Special Sales Department" at the address above.

Beyond the Covenant/ James F. Gaines -- 1st ed.
ISBN 978-0-9981721-6-3

To John, the Continuator and Initiator

Acknowledgements

"For More Than Their Souls" appeared originally in *Riverside Currents,* "Beyond the Covenant" in *Rappahannock Review,* "The Sheepskin Jacket" in *Riverside Echoes,* "Middle Management" in *Riverside Reflections,* "Diogenes in King George County" in *River Tides,* and "War Games" in *The Virginia Writers Club 100th Anniversary Anthology.*

Cover Art: "U-Boat After Torpedoing British Cargo Ship," Adolf Bock, 1941. By arrangement with Shutterstock.

Table of Contents

For More than Their Souls   7

Beyond the Covenant   49

The Sheepskin Jacket   71

Middle Management   83

First Light   101

War Games   133

Under the Lens   151

Diogenes in King George County   171

The Witches of Okemos   177

For More than Their Souls

"Père Rémy!" shouted the sailor up on the foresail yard, "Look, Father, there is your Martinique at last!" Père Rémy blinked his eyes, trying to adjust to the dazzling light up on deck, and squinted in the direction that Lebeau had pointed. Sure enough, a tall island of iridescent green was looming up out of the waves to starboard, and the crew was taking in sail as fast as it could to prepare for a careful entry into the still unseen harbor. Having secured his section of the canvas, Lebeau swung peacefully, his bare brown feet on the ropes, waiting for his mates to finish before they moved up the ratlines to the next sail. "Soon you will be ashore, the guest of the famous Père Labat, who will teach you all about the missions. And let me tell you, he will not let you leave until you have tasted the finest cuisine in the Antilles."

"And what will you do when you are ashore, Lebeau? I hope you will not waste your wages in all the wrong places." Rémy had grown quite fond of the spry fellow from Nantes who had assisted him in preparing for Mass on board the *Marie-Hélène* during their eighty-day crossing.

"Me, Father? Oh, no! I am courting the most beautiful daughter of a ship's chandler in Basse-Terre. Her father has no sons and will be most happy to have me take up the trade. You can make a good life in these ports, if you know how to be industrious and discreet." A snicker came from his mates further down the yard, who had just finished and were listening to the conversation with evident amusement.

"Lebeau can no longer keep up with our drinking, Father, and he seeks a soft life now. He will become a Monsieur Pantoufle!"

Père Rémy himself had to smile at that jest, but Lebeau pouted and shot back, "Better a comfortable little slipper for me than the old leather you will be looking for tonight!" -- which caused the whole gang to roar for a moment, before they clambered up to the foretopsail.

The priest stared dreamily at the island and could already see the festoons of multicolored flowers hanging in the forests. He thought to himself, "I will see little enough of those towns and their comforts. For me, the wilderness of the interior, and the rough life of the poor Indians I shall bring to God. I will share what they have, and they will share my faith."

He was greeted at the dock by a plump, red-faced Dutchman, respectfully holding his hat over his paunch. "Père Rémy, welcome to Martinique! I am to bring you to Père Labat, who I have de honor to serve. I am Schmidt, overseer to his ... missionary gardens. If you would please climb in de cart, de men are already loading your luggage."

The trip through up from the port into the hillsides was slow and pleasant, the swaying gait of the two oxen yoked to the cart allowing the priest to get his land legs gradually after so long a time at sea. The people along the roadside were extremely deferential, and Creoles at a couple of homes along the way rushed out to offer Père Rémy little gifts of sweets and fruits, but the givers limited themselves to fleeting welcomes and did not seem as anxious as Rémy would have expected to engage the overseer in conversation.

The quick tropical twilight had overtaken them on route and it was almost pitch-black when the plodding oxen brought them to Père Labat's home. Père Rémy almost gasped in surprise, for instead of the cozy, vine-covered presbytère he had imagined, here was a full-scale planter's *habitation*, raised up on short brick piers from the ground and surrounded by a long veranda. So tired was he that he recalled little of the jovial greeting by his thick-set, energetic host, and after several courses of a dinner that didn't seem to end, he must have fallen asleep between glasses of bordeaux, because he awoke very late the next morning, the sun already streaming in through the shutters of his room, where, to his great surprise, everything had already been unpacked and set in order.

"Ah, you see," said Père Labat, entering with a tray of coffee and fresh breads, "You are a heavy sleeper, as are all who arrive from a long sea voyage. I and my helpers have been creeping around like mice this morning arranging your things, and you will find all your clothes freshly aired and ironed."

"I am dreadfully sorry to keep you so long, Father. I merely..."

"Tut, tut, my dear Père Rémy, here you are free to sleep in. *Faites la grasse matinée* as long as you care to, and also do not be surprised if one takes a nap in the noontime heat." He sat down on the side of the bed as Rémy sipped some coffee and broke a surprisingly good brioche. "You see, we are in the tropics here, and we must devise our own ways of doing things. You cannot rely on the archbishop's deacon to give you help, because he is far away in Québec! Yes, that's right, if you want to communicate with your bishop, you have to find a boat heading for France (no question of finding one here that goes to Canada!), then arrange to transfer the message to a boat for Québec, and once that has been done, wait a mere eighteen months or so until the reply arrives by the same route. That is supposing, of course, that the bishop or the archdeacon or both have not decided to return to France themselves, for instructions or a rest, in which case you may grow quite old before you receive an answer. You will find that in the colonial Missions, you must exercise considerable initiative and enterprise to survive."

And enterprise there certainly was, as Rémy eventually found out. Not all at once, for he continued to feel very weary for days after his arrival, sleeping well into the morning and taking advantage of the breakfast in bed offered by his host, emerging in the afternoon to explore the house and especially Père Labat's remarkably well-stocked library. ("It costs me much pain and effort," his host complained, "Each book must be continually cleaned, pressed, and often rebound in this humidity.") He spent several days completing his letters home to family, friends, and superiors in the Franciscan order, letters that were whisked away by Schmidt as he made his thrice-weekly trip to market in the capital, his cart loaded with produce. For when Rémy was able to finally explore farther than the house, he found a thriving plantation. Fields stretched for miles around in every direction, and down the road past Schmidt's cottage, towards nightfall, he could see the smoke of what must have been a slave compound rising above the trees. He had little notion of the slaves' lives, for the house Negroes that served at the *habitation* seemed fit enough, dressed in cast-off but well-maintained European clothes and perpetually sweeping, cleaning, polishing, or out back in the detached kitchen, stoking the ovens and preparing rather amazing meals for Père Labat, Schmidt, and himself. Père Labat recommended that they visit some of the neighbors and Rémy discovered that all the planters, both the pale Europeans and the Creoles, whose *café au lait* complexions showed their mixed ancestry, enjoyed a similar level of luxury. He marveled at how well his host, who adhered punctually to his pastoral duties and kept up a heavy correspondence with people all over the islands, as well as in Canada and Europe, was able to manage such an operation. At the end of three weeks, Rémy at last had shaken off the effects of what his colleague called a *changement d'air* and insisted that he was well enough to help Père Labat with the daily Mass.

While Père Labat adjusted his surplice and stared into the mirror at his bulbous nose, he hummed a native tune that Père Rémy did not recognize.

"I am too new to the Antilles," Rémy thought. He stared out the window at the plantation his host had carved out of the lush wilderness. Orderly rows of sugar cane stretched downhill towards the sea, and further on, in a patch of indigo, slaves slowly tended to the new crop. "How is it that you come to have so many . . . servants?" he asked the older man.

"The slaves?" Labat turned brusquely as though jarred from a pleasant thought. "I bought the first ones with ten *livres* I inherited from an uncle, as soon as I stepped off the boat. An excellent investment. I now have almost forty. It makes life much easier, I can tell you that."

"Don't you find it difficult to reconcile such ease with your vows? Understand that I ask this because I am a newcomer who must face these decisions, and not because I wish to criticize," Rémy added sheepishly.

"You Recollects," snorted the Benedictine, "Always tripping up over that poverty Saint Francis left in your way. Be reasonable. This is a reasonable world and a reasonable island, despite what you may think. Here those slaves are part of the real world. You must attend to more than the soul, but to the body as well. You find them on the dock, waiting to be sold, staring straight ahead like dolts, perfectly idle with their arms held in a little wooden yoke. You can buy them cheap or you can buy them dear. If you do the former, you may produce some useful harvests and contribute to the prosperity of his Most Christian Majesty's colonies. Spend too much money and you will not be able to afford that fine Saint-Emilion we enjoyed last night. Also," he added, turning to show off the immaculate vestments, "You will soon find yourself going about in ragged linen."

"I must agree that your establishment here is the talk of the Foreign Missions. Everyone considers you an absolute expert and a model priest. I must agree that your farm is most impressive."

"I have reason to be proud of it. But listen," Labat half-whispered as he drew close to his guest, "You know what gives me the greatest pleasure of all?"

"The tropical fruits? The coconuts? The diabolical peppers?"

"Not at all!" laughed Labat, with the jollity of a *père Noël*, "My herb garden. It is over there, surrounded by a hedge. Brought the seeds with me all the way from Brittany. I have lavender, sage, thyme, oh the modest little purple blossoms on my thyme when it blooms! I sit in there and in a few seconds I forget all about Martinique. The regular little squares of parsley and basil transport me back to some quiet cloister in the provinces. The order! The charm of it all!" He smiled benignly, but then a glint appeared in one eye. "Of course, I have medicinals, too. The only ones on this side of the island. Many people come for them. I make them pay, just for the cost of replacement, of course." He winked.

Rémy's admiration swelled in him like a cough that he would have liked to stifle. "You deserve your reputation. I salute you."

"I know what people say at the Missions, and don't think I am going to let it all die out without making the most of it. When I do return to France, I intend to publish a book. Already I have journals full of the most useful observations. Everything from the flora and fauna to the plans for constructing a sugar mill. But it is almost time for Mass and we do not want to be late."

They emerged into the sunlight and Rémy could instantly feel it piercing through his vestments and settling on his skin. The March air, so unlike the icy March of his native Dauphiné, was alive with colorful birds and exotic song. It was more like a holiday than a mission to the unevangelized world, and he could not imagine the horrors of martyrdom he had read about in the monastery, the edifying abnegation and torture that ushered Christ into the hearts of the savages. Here he was with the celebrated Père Labat, supposedly learning all the lessons he would need for his ordeals, and his visit had consisted of little else but visits to sparkling houses, where planters kept birds that were not even to be found in the Jardin des Plantes and ate meals that seemed like something out of a novelist's wildest imagination, where even the barefoot pirates wore costly shirts and plumed hats above their leather breeches. And amid all this profusion something undefinable and unstated seemed to be missing.

At Mass, Rémy prayed for enlightenment, but since the word *lumières* was taking on such a nasty connotation lately, thanks to the Anglomaniac ravings of that Monsieur Voltaire and his cohorts, he asked the Almighty for "éclaircissement" instead. His introspection was a marked (and probably rare) exception at the ceremony, where Labat's parishioners, wearing the warmest of smiles, almost tapped their feet with pleasure as their pastor marched them through the Mass and finally gave them a booming benediction. His boisterous tones shooed them out the doors before the tropical sun further heated the white walls of his oven-shaped sanctuary.

Labat walked briskly back up the road on the way home and the younger Recollect had difficulty keeping up with him. Rémy spied a parcel under Labat's arm and remembered that a barefoot fellow with a sword at his side had given it to him at the church door. Labat caught his guest staring at the package and explained, "Butter. Dutch butter. Twenty-five pounds kept on ice and taken off a ship from Rotterdam only last evening. Kept on ice all the way. The man who passed it to me, La Varnière, is a pious buccaneer who never misses Mass when he is ashore and always brings me the most useful things from the merchantmen he falls in with. You may have noticed the fine bell on our church? It used to toll over Maracaibo, but the lads took it and a good deal else away forever and the Spaniards will never miss it. Fine cloth, books, preserves, even a most useful telescope that once belonged to an English captain -- they never fail to provide for us, these gentlemen of the sea. And it would be a great mistake to assume that they have no need for spiritual guidance. Let's hurry a bit more, this butter is starting to melt."

    Rémy was now rushing to keep up both physically and mentally. "I can see I have much to learn," he panted.

    "You do well to listen. The whole Church would do well, because their policies are far from realistic in this part of creation. The pirates are essential, and one will soon see that their benevolence will permit the entire religious work of the Antilles to subsist without a penny's subsidy from the Church or the Crown. All at the expense of the miscreants."

Rémy decided not to ask whether the Spanish of Maracaibo were also newly designated miscreants. Instead he asked whether the windfall donations would also support the missions among the Indians.

"You may be surprised to learn that I have recommended the abolition of all missionary work among the Caribs. Yes, I am sure you are shocked because you dreamed of converting them all. But let me tell you it's quite impossible. For one thing there are very few left, and most that remain are moldering away in disease-ridden hovels in the hills. There are a handful who remember now the ways and crafts of the past, and I have a devil of a time finding a few families to trade with. More of that later. For the time being, suffice it to say that they are quite incapable of becoming Christians. Yes, they are willing to let you baptize them one minute because it seems a good thing to do, and five minutes later you will find your converts coupled in the most atrocious sodomy because that also seems a good thing to do."

Rémy agonized now, and it was hard for him to say if it was in the lungs or in the heart. "You mean it is hopeless to try to bring the all-illuminating example of Christ's passion to these unfortunates?"

"Quite in vain. Oh, passion they understand, all right. But they are totally unwilling to change their lazy, sensuous ways. And yet, for all that, they are quite attached to their freedom, and even to a kind of pride. If you so much as look askance at a Carib, it is as good as beating him, and if you beat him you might as well kill him."

"Is that why I see none on the plantations?"

"Yes. They will not work, either for profit, for love, or by compulsion. Unlike the blacks."

The pace was slowing a bit as the two priests neared the house. Puffing, Rémy was at last able to catch his breath. "On the boat, I heard many things about the blacks, some of them most ugly. One gentleman asserted that to beat a black . . ."

"It's absolutely true," nodded Labat, "To beat a slave is like feeding him." He rushed off to his cool-box with the butter.

That evening, Rémy was finishing his devotions in the privacy of the tiny guest room, when he heard a commotion. A woman's feet had run in down the hallway, there had been a lot of whispering, and he thought he heard the word "sorcier." Then Labat's stocky body was thumping towards the back door and something metallic was banging on the walls. Rémy rushed out and tried to follow through the ink-black night towards the slave quarters behind the kitchen. After stumbling against and over he knew not what, he finally made it to a cabin door at the same time as a couple of slaves carrying blazing *flambeaux*. In the light of the torches, he saw Labat, holding a rifle that was pointed into the building. Inside, a very pregnant slave-girl lay softly moaning on a wooden cot, while over her hovered a tall black man unlike any he had seen since he landed. The man's face and naked torso were painted with something that looked like ashes and blood. In one hand he held a feather fan and in the other a horrid talisman made of bones that clattered as he chanted something in an African language that even most of the slaves appeared not to know. Indifferent to the barrel of the gun that Labat held almost to his temple, the witch doctor softly and insistently muttered the same words over and over. Reversing his weapon, Labat knocked him out of his trance with a blow from the stock across his face.

The black was silent a second and Rémy could not imagine what was going through his head. He opened his lips as if to speak, but before he could, Labat hit him again. "Do not dare say the name of the devil in my plantation, you worshipper of Satan!" Suddenly the usually jolly face of the Benedictine had taken on a crimson glow, redder than that of the shaman, who was spitting blood and broken teeth, trying to breathe and rise up at the same time. Labat kicked him furiously in his exposed ribs, and then again, further down, as he rolled to the ground. "Satan, I shall crush you. Crush you! I will teach you with your black magic. Black magic! Take this!" Labat was smashing the stock down on the man's back now, as he wretched and cried in pain. Rémy was too revolted to look on any longer, and as he averted his face, he glanced upon those of the slaves, clustering now near the door of the cabin. Most had a stunned, shocked look, some, like him, were turning aside, but two women were leaping up and down, flailing their arms and screaming something -- it must have been in Creole -- that the priest could not understand.

    Labat suddenly gripped the Recollect's arm firmly and, over his shoulder, ordered two stout men to tie the villain to the pole that held the clothesline. To another he barked, "Find Schmidt!" He appeared startlingly lucid and held the butt of the rifle out so that it would not rub blood on his clothes. "This is my overseer's fault and it is he who will administer the punishment."

The thought of any more beating made Rémy's head whirl. "I . . . I must excuse myself. My nerves . . . "

Labat gripped him with both hands now. "No, my brother. You *will* witness this. It is unthinkable that these slaves should see a white man turn aside at such a time. Take on a stern countenance. Say your breviary if you must, but if you so much as shed a tear, I will have you on the first ship out from Basse-Terre and back to a cell in Dauphiné before you can sneeze. Show some virile virtue or you'll wish you had!"

Labat left Rémy for a minute to compose himself, as the fat Hollander Schmidt came lumbering up the path. "Ave Maria," Rémy began, and then checked himself. "No, not yet, I will need Her further on, for sure. Shall I run and shame myself? No, think, you are French, French. You cannot suffer others to laugh at you, that above all. What is happening is the devil's work. Oh, God, I wish I had never come here."

Suddenly, he found he was clutching his breviary. "I am a Franciscan," he remembered, as calm flooded the troubled landscape of his conscience. He looked at the man tied to the pole. "I am obliged by my order to stop this cruelty. Mercy. Here. Now. Even now."

He tensed his muscles, set his jaw, strode over to where Labat was whispering to his superintendent and placed his hand on Labat's bear-like shoulder. "My dear brother, as a Christian, I must say . . . "

Labat cut him off by booming, "Of course, there you are. Worthy, as I knew you would be. Courage!" He picked Rémy up like a toy and planted him square in front of the tall slave.

"You cannot . . . " began the Recollect. But immediately Labat began to harangue his slaves in Creole. It was useless. Rémy wished at least that he had learned the language well enough to know what Labat was saying, but all he could grasp were disparate words about sorcery, devils, evil, repeated with emphasis, and finally at the end, the sentence: *trois cent coups*. Right away, Schmidt began to whip the slave.

Rémy again mustered the determination to protest and asked "How can you do this?"

"You are right of course, this creature is not my property, for he belongs to Destouches down the road. Yet in such cases it is the responsibility of the local owner to give the first correction, after which the rascal's master will give another. I insist on observing this custom, all the more so because it is a matter of a serious spiritual crime. Remember that in France also blasphemers are still, thank God, being broken on the wheel and burned on the slow fire. I wish that were true here as well, but we must remember that this brute is also an investment, and the purchaser is entitled to try to redeem as much wealth as possible to repay his risk." All at once, he interrupted his homily and shouted to Schmidt, "Fifty-five, fifty-five, not fifty-nine, you fool, do not try to shorten his punishment by a stroke, and put some life into that whip or I shall have you thrown in jail over that little matter we know about."

Schimdt scowled behind his disheveled whiskers. The Hollander had been before the mast and probably still had too much of the sailor in him to enjoy a flogging, too much of the mutineer to apply the lashes as he should. "Fifty-six!" he intoned, and leaned into the blow a bit more, waiting until Labat was distracted to slack off or forget his count again.

Rémy studied the face of the black man. It was not distorted with hate, like the faces he had seen at executions back home, nor was it lax with resignation. The eyes were glazed with what might have been a memory, and it was evident that the wretch was patiently conserving every ounce of energy to pour into that concentration, slowly and almost lovingly conjuring up from inside something that was not a devil at all. But it was only a matter of time. At one hundred and twelve lashes, even the kind Schmidt had been doling out, the welts on the back began to break and rivelets of blood began streaming down the shining flesh. The overseer was now trying to concentrate the strokes on the shoulders, to spare as much skin as possible, but Labat ordered some of the onlookers to cut away the criminal's pants and told Schmidt to strike all the way down to the knees.

    At two hundred and forty lashes, the entire back from neck to knees was an open wound and each additional blow brought a fresh splattering of blood. Rémy's robes were covered with tiny red spots, but somehow Labat managed to dodge all the spray and to remain untouched as he leafed through his breviary. Incredibly, the slave had remained conscious to this point, but now his neck suddenly bent forward and he collapsed. A gurgling noise came from his throat and it was evident that he would smother if the ordeal continued. "Piment!" commanded Labat, and an old woman moved forward with a jar and began to daub something on what had been the African's back. With a jolt he came to and, his body rigid as a violin string, he uttered a scream so exquisite and eternal that it might have come from one of the damned at the Last Judgment.

"In the name of God . . . " muttered Rémy.

"Crushed peppers," explained Labat. "Revives them instantly, if they can be revived. And an excellent preventative for gangrene." The Benedictine went on about the cultivation of this delicacy, but Rémy's attention was all on the scene before him. Racing toward three hundred, Schmidt was skipping lashes now by fours and fives as Labat spoke. His arm was growing so tired and heavy that he was hitting hard despite himself and he stopped twice to vomit, hoping that he could control the next lashes.

At last the end came and Labat ordered a fresh coat of pepper sauce to be spread on the sorcerer's back by way of medication. The women cried as they patted it onto the writhing form that had become a positively unearthly scarlet.

"Would you be needing a little *eau de vie*?" Labat called after Rémy as the latter raced for his room, but there was no answer. The Benedictine smiled knowingly. He had a good glass of rum in his chamber and quickly fell into a sleep that was free of demons and magic.

The next morning, after Rémy despaired of getting any rest, he found Labat bustling around the little settlement yard. The pole that held the clothesline had been freshly washed and the ground around freshly raked over and sanded so that no trace of blood remained. Rémy refused breakfast and, when he saw Labat heading for the serenity of his herb garden, made his way to the shack where Schmidt lived. He went straight into the filthy place and shook the plump Dutchman till he awoke. "Son of a bitch . . . Oh, Reverend Father . . . " the overseer mumbled. "Never mind that," Rémy cut in, "That man last night . . ."

"Dat slave, 'Tit Philippe? Back to his master. He'll live, I tink. His master won't whip him again until next Friday, if he's so lucky." He rolled over and tried to go back to sleep.

"Who was he?" Rémy persisted.

"Medicine man, sure enough," snorted Schmidt. "You know, de voo-doo, de gris-gris. Long time ago in Guinea maybe he was big medicine chief. That girl he make a spell on, dat his daughter, born here in the island. She was real sick with dat baby coming." The Hollander gave a little chuckle. "Maybe dat magic do her some good. She is today good, her baby good too. What you tink, father?"

Rémy scowled. "Devil worship is no laughing matter, my man. It can get you in a lot of trouble."

Schmidt shrugged. "Not me, I tink, fahter, not me. I go no more to the Protestant *temple*. Got me baptized in Catholic Church, go to Mass, give in collection plate each time. Look." He dragged a crucifix from a table beside the bed, where it had lain beside a half-finished glass of some liquor and a smelly pipe. "Now I go back schlaffen, please, good day."

Father Rémy arranged to visit another of his order in an outlying village so that he could be away from Father Labat for a number of days. When he returned, he thought he could forgive him. Rémy found him beaming as usual on his doorstep and returned Labat's embrace with good heart. "I have arranged quite a meal for your 'homecoming'," the elder friar explained. Two days ago I shot an excellent goose, and this morning my buccaneers brought me three fine dorado fish, which my cook has baked with limes. And here we have to water it down ... an excellent bottle of Entre-deux-Mers just off the boat."

Rémy refrained from asking what boat. He accepted Labat for what he was and any time he felt his smile slipping or his tongue becoming tense, he said a pair of short devotional prayers his fellow Recollect had taught him for just such a purpose. "I shall get used to these islands," he congratulated himself.

That evening before he retired to his chamber, Labat looked in on Rémy and said with a twinkle in his eye, "I have a real treat for you tomorrow. We shall go to visit some of your cherished Caribs and see how they really are."

Rémy said a great many prayers that night and fell sound asleep. He was awakened by a strange noise and found to his astonishment that it was still the middle of the night, with no hint of dawn discernible over the eastern hills. The house itself seemed quiet, but keening his ears, Rémy detected a rhythmic thump, accompanied by a sort of undulating wail, coming from somewhere behind the slave quarters. Slipping into his robe, he set out across the yard, past the darkened huts, and through the fields toward a distance light. He hoped the foliage whipping at his sandal-clad feet was not hot pepper plants, which he had heard torment the hands of the harvesters, or even worse, indigo, which works a slow poison deep into the veins of those who handle it. The light grew nearer and he could make out gyrating shapes around an open-air fire. He drew closer, hiding in the shrubbery, and saw that the dancers were slaves, apparently the slaves of the pious Father Labat. But if they had piety it had rubbed off now, for their dance was more explicitly lewd than anything Rémy could have imagined. The dark bodies lifted their legs and shook their breasts and genitals, rounded their hips in a sinful mime of copulation, even pressed against each other, sex to sex, bringing their warm skins into a contact that could only result in abandonment. Rémy felt one moment like fleeing back to the security of the house, another moment like striding out from his hiding place into the clearing, crucifix held high, admonishing the wayward children to fall down before their true Lord. He did neither, but continued to watch. "The Kalamba," he said to himself, recalling the name of this orgy, which he had heard on his passage from the Old World. "It is awful in its desperation and in its power. Perhaps," he realized, "Perhaps it is how they manage to live with all this. Perhaps it is at least a part of their secret. It is fortunate that Père Labat does not know his own . . . creatures are behaving this way." Noiselessly, Rémy began to circle around the fire to reach the shortest path back to the plantation, but as he groped among the tree limbs, he suddenly saw about ten yards away from him, hunched next to rock but in full view of the dancers, a form that could only be Père Labat. Seen only from behind, the priest appeared to be giving rapt attention to the spectacle. Rémy felt sick and ashamed as he sneaked back to the big house.

"You seem out of sorts," the older priest observed, frowning, as he surprised Père Rémy in the library the next morning. The Recollect shuffled some papers over the letter he had been writing and stammered, "Yes, well, you see, it is that I have now done all that is necessary to prepare for my missionary duties, and I am feeling guilty over enjoying your hospitality so long, and eager to get into the work for which I came."

"I really think you may be wasting your time. If you allow me, I am sure I can arrange for you to take over the next vacant curate's position, either here or on Guadeloupe. As curate, you will see that you can deal more easily with the spiritual matters that lie closest to your heart."

"I am aware of your opinions of the futility of evangelizing the savages, but I must insist on keeping to the engagements I have already made."

"Very well, I have set up a little expedition for us into the back country."

"You propose to accompany me? I assure you I am able to manage on my own. No need to distract you."

"On the contrary, I would consider it a breach of duty as well as hospitality if I did not make sure that you are completely settled in your new environment before I left you alone."

"In that case, I am grateful to accept." Lord, forgive my lies, he said to himself, for he knew he was actually very troubled that Père Labat had decided to come along. He had hoped to leave as much distance as he could between the eminent colonist and himself, especially in view of the damning letters he was about to send off. But now he realized he must persevere a little longer. What was it Lebeau had said, back on the *Marie-Hélène*? Oh yes, one can get along well on the islands if one is discrete; how right he was.

The way to the Carib village at the south end of the island was long and tortuous. Labat had borrowed a trio of nags from one of his neighbors and the priests set forth on their mounts, with the extra horse carrying some packages that the Dutchman brought along, wrapped in oilcloth. The path led through lush, liana-festooned valleys, over ridges where the sea air cleared the nostrils of the tropic stench of perfume and leaf-mold, past occasional isolated cottages among which Rémy was astonished to see blonde little English boys playing ball or bronzed mestizos left over from the Spanish conquest. As they neared their destination they skirted magnificent beaches of sand as pure as the verges of Eden and caught sight of a sea whose wanton beauty only caught fire when it kissed the uninhibited land.

Labat took advantage of the trip to display his encyclopedic knowledge of beast and bird, of all that grew or crawled or slunk or hovered in the island. Remembering Sancho Pansa, Rémy was tempted to exclaim, "You speak just like a book." However, he left his fellow priest to his scientific crusade and tried to fix in his mind the perfection of raw form and color so that sometime in the future, under different skies, he could recapture this vision in Christian love for the benefit of others who had

The Secret Diary
of
Ewan Macrae

is available on
Amazon.com
and Kindle

jahill.mail@gmail.com

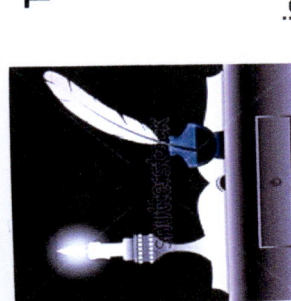

The historian tells you what happened.
The novelist tells you how it felt.

E. L. Doctorow

never seen the imprint of God's hand fresh upon the earth or been filled with the intoxicating, wild hope it instilled.

When they reached the small clearing containing the Carib huts, the natives laughingly rushed to lay hands of welcome on their guests. Rémy had expected a withered people, bowed by disease and crushed by poverty, and was unprepared for the radiance of the Indians. True, they did not resemble the illustrations in travel books he had seen, where Indians for some reason always had a distinctly Grecian deportment. They were foreign in shape and color and sound and smell from all the people he had known, and yet the Caribs' naked skin was full of life and taut with enjoyment, not the way Europeans see themselves, but the way they wish they could be. They could have been some kind of perfect, animated machines, were it not for their child-like giggling, their clear-eyed curiosity, and their wonderful, unmechanical, dangerous sense of faith. "Here could be my calling," Rémy exulted.

"Help me with these," called Labat, who was removing something from the bundles on the pack-horse. Rémy took the object that was passed to him and saw that it was a small keg of rum. Labat had seven others on the horse, along with a couple of rusty rifles and a small keg of gunpowder. Already the sick feeling was returning to the Recollect.

To Rémy's misery, Labat seemed perfectly conversant in the Carib language, and in no time he had them passing around wooden cups of rum. As Labat bantered away, Rémy tried to huddle with the women and children of the village, thinking that they at least would not become corrupted, but the cups began to pass from the men to the women and from the oldest to the youngest. When Rémy, with tears in his eyes, tried to urge them to pass back the cups without drinking, they thought it was a game and whirled him around, saying sweet, cooing words to him in their language, and bringing the despised liquid to his own lips.

Labat, who had already consumed at least half a cask himself, was utterly content. "You see," he said, "how simple they are. Like a lot of naughty little children. Watch this, it is going to be good. When the women drink they do the funniest things!"

In fact, one of the natives had brought a woman to sit in Labat's lap and two others were dancing in front of him in the most lascivious manner.

"You must be mad, my friend. It is dangerous to give these simple people things like rum and those guns you have brought. I must protest."

"Not at all," the older said, as he fondled the Indian woman's breast, "I wanted to show you how these savages really are. The guns will buy us a little insight and pleasure -- perfectly excusable under the circumstances. I have only brought enough powder to allow them a little hunting and some specimen-collecting for my studies. I intend to make them totally dependent on us for more powder, and that way, they will do whatever we like, won't they, Schmidt?"

The leering Dutchman emerged from behind a hut, holding two children firmly by the hand. "Shall I begin now?" he asked Père Labat. The younger priest did not want to think about what he meant.

Père Rémy whirled around, vainly looking for help. All the Caribs were by now completely at the mercy of the Europeans, stumbling around the encampment with cups of rum and mumbling some jargon that only they could understand. "I must take action," Rémy thought, "I must not let them fall into the hands of this monster! But how could I awaken them? How could I force them to save themselves?" His eyes fell on the small powder keg sitting by the horses. Perhaps if he tossed it into the fire, the explosion would bring the Caribs to their senses, or at least send them flying into the forest in fright. He began staggering toward the horses, dizzy from the effects of fatigue, rum, and fear.

Père Labat watched him idly as he played with the Indian woman. "You look wretched, my friend," he laughed, "Better restore yourself with some of the fresh water in that brown jug on the back pack." It seemed like a good idea. The Recollect could barely keep himself upright now, and he drank greedily from the jug to give himself strength for his plan.

It didn't seem to work. As he picked up the powder keg, he felt more exhausted and more woozy than ever. He had to concentrate on holding on, as a kind of numbness invaded his fingers. Père Labat laughed at him. "Yes, my hearty, bring over that powder and set it right by me. What, you don't want to do what I say? You wouldn't be so stupid as to throw it into the fire, would you? Look how he walks right past me without responding, Schmidt. Oh dear, I don't think he is going to make it. He is swaying. He begins to stumble. Clumsy idiot, and now he falls!"

He awoke upright when something hot passed back and forth in front of his face and an odd smell came to his nostrils. As his eyes focused with difficulty, he saw Père Labat standing in front of him with a torch and realized with horror that the smell came from his own moustache and eyebrows that were being singed. Outside the light of the torch, it was night, but he could make out what seemed to be other torches around the encampment. "Welcome back, most reverend Father," mocked Labat, "You are just in time for the grand finale. Let's have another one, Schmidt!"

The Dutchman spilled some rum over one of several stupefied Caribs he had lined up in a row in front of him. When the tottering Indian reached Labat, he lowered his torch and ignited the savage's rum-soaked loincloth. After a few astonished seconds, the Carib gave a desperate scream and ran into the nearest hut, but that, too, was immediately ablaze and man and home were consumed together.

Rémy gave what should have been a lurch forward, intent on strangling the man in the black cassock, in spite of any vows he had ever taken, but found he could not even flinch. Not only were his hands sternly tied to a stick above his head with leather thongs, but his muscles would not obey the mind's commands.

He remembered the last few minutes before he lost consciousness and suddenly gasped.

"Ah, now you begin to understand, no? A little something from my herb garden will make you pay attention while I make my remonstrance, Père Rémy, for you have behaved very badly, yes, badly. Continual debauchery since the moment you set foot on the island, lechery, defiling of innocent native children. I have duly documented all this in letters to the appropriate authorities, my man. My corsair friends have already sent them on, faster than any royal mail. What, you shake your head and disagree? Then you should have taken more time to say goodbye to your shipmates and to get to know people in the town, instead of lingering slothfully in your room for a month. You see, you have no witnesses, no one to corroborate your side of the story."

"My... letters," he managed to murmur.

"Your letters, oh of course, right here!" And he pulled a thick packet out of his pocket and threw it into the campfire, where it disappeared in a red flare. "I suppose lazy Schmidt must have forgotten to send them in the post. Shame on you, Schmidt."

Rémy looked for the Dutchman and saw him in the distant light of another flaming hut, fastening thongs on the wrists of one of the children, the other end looped into a noose around the neck of the child in front of her.

"Since you are wicked and wasteful enough to destroy this whole village, I cannot help but take advantage of a few little survivors, for whom I have several errands," explained Père Labat with a flourish. "I should have told you that these creatures, like the blacks, are useful for far more than their souls."

"I will see you are punished!"

"Punish me! But how, my dear friend? Since you died in the same conflagration with those you were to convert. Look, your face already shows signs of the fire, and as soon as Schmidt bestirs himself to open the other keg of rum, we will anoint you most fittingly in a slightly alcoholic extreme unction and be on our way."

Rémy struggled until he began to grow faint again, but just as he was losing consciousness, he saw a vision of an arc of dark wood flashing through the firelight and crashing into Père Labat's head. He felt like he was being jostled and was sick, but the jostling continued. He tried to speak but couldn't. Somehow he knew he was being carried, still bound, on a pair of enormous shoulders, crashing through the foliage of the forest. Behind him he heard an explosion, then another, and heard something tear through the branches nearby. Just as he was fading into darkness again, he looked down at the dark expanse of a man's naked back, a black man, and the skin was criss-crossed by a traces of a scarred embroidery, faintly tinged with the red hue of crushed peppers.

Rémy awoke in a room, under a sheet, under the gaze of a black woman whose face looked familiar, although he was sure he had never met her. "Who are you?"

"Me? I am called Jeannette. No formalities. No use to say 'vous' here, Father, in this place everyone is 'tu'."

"And what is this place? I remember a man..."

"The man was my father, Tit Philippe, who brought you here and watched over you for nearly a whole day until you looked better and the poison started to weaken. And the place is a whorehouse, La Maison Rouge, and I am a whore, at your service," she giggled.

"But how...," he stammered, "Where is..."

"Don't worry, Father, just a little joke. I would not hurt you. A whorehouse is the best place in the island to hide, since no one bothers a whore as long as she has a man in her bed. Then she is working, *tout est normal*. The

Master Labat sold me to the owner of this house several years ago, after he had tried me out himself. Now I am one of the best girls in the house and even the matron has to listen when I have my say," she gloated, as she arranged the scarlet scarf that covered her coiffe.

"Where are my clothes?" he said, shocked to find himself nearly naked under the covers. "Good Lord, my superiors..."

"Oh, we had to throw them in the fire. Père Labat and his men could recognize you too easily and have already searched the town for anyone in a cassock. Oh, don't worry, and don't move," she added, seeing him becoming more agitated. "Pépé could not kill Labat with his hoe because it broke. Pépé was not surprised because Labat is protected by the powers of the Blue Devil. He was just able to cut loose you and some children before Labat and Bedaine (we call Schmidt that because of his belly) came after him with guns. They did not see who he was, and that was why he had to go back to the village so soon, for the sake of Talinda and the baby. Talinda is my sister. You seen her when Pépé was whipped. They been watching you for a long time because they were worried that a Monpé, a holy father, would fall under the powers of the Blue Devil, making things even worse. Pépé followed Bedaine when he saw you had gone with the Master carrying guns and rum."

"I must get out into the town and send messages."

"Pas question! Everyone in town is looking for you, and the Master's pirates are looking on other islands, too. If they spot you, you will not last five minutes. First, we will wait until you are completely well in two or three days. Then, I will dress you in a nice wig and some clothes left behind some time ago by a client in a hurry. Then, I will introduce you to an Englishman I know who will take you to another island. You see, we thought everything out."

Rémy reflected for a while in his bed, while Jeanette straightened out the room and prepared to go out to the market for some groceries. As she was about to go out the door, he turned towards her and asked, "Why have you done this for me, since I -- I am ashamed to say it -- did nothing for your family?"

"It is a matter of the spirit," she said, sitting at his bedside with a serious expression. "But not just the spirit, the body, too. There is really no difference, or only a difference we think we see, but is not there. If Pépé were here he could explain it better because he is wise. You Monpés think the spirit is always good, but it is not. There are bad spirits like the Blue Devil -- they are not bad to everyone, but they can only do bad things. The good and the bad spirits try to get the bodies of people and animals to work for them, to do what they are saying."

"Just the contrary of why I came here," Rémy muttered.

"What? Oh, don't interrupt. Where was I? Oh yes, the good and bad spirits try to control the bodies in this world, especially with all kinds of magic and spells that cause things to change in strange ways. The more bodies they rule over, the more spell power they have. It grows on the minds of the people who come into their kingdoms. Already the power of Labat is strong with the Blue Devil, not only because he is clever and evil, but also because he is a Monpé, and if you join him and two Monpés serve the Blue Devil, Pépé thinks the island will forever be in his power. So even though you were weak and did not understand, he had to take you away from Labat's power."

"But what of me now? I am a man without anything if I leave God. And surely God would not want me unless I can find some way to bring that awful Labat to justice. What will become of me?"

"Who knows, Monpé," sighed Jeanette wistfully. "Perhaps, without your cassock, you can find a home here in the islands. Do you know a trade? There are always too many scoundrels here and never enough people with an honest trade."

"When I was young, I helped my father in the bakery. I suppose I can still bake a decent loaf if I can find some good flour and an oven."

"Voilà, mister baker, your fortune is made! You can choose your home anywhere in the Antilles. Perhaps you will marry a Creole girl and start a family. For if you have no woman here, people will wonder, and then they might start to remember the holy father who disappeared. It is better to start a new life and to be like other men. Perhaps," Jeannette added with a serious look, "Father Labat will fall into your hands someday. Perhaps you will see him on the dock without his pirates or maybe he will even walk into your shop. Then you will have to choose whether you will have revenge or a peaceful life. And maybe you will never have to make that choice."

"Go on to the market, now," replied Rémy, thoughtfully. "Don't worry about me leaving. I will do as you say. And thank you. Thank you all." He settled back in bed after she left and wished at first that he had his breviary, a comfortable anchor to lay his hand on, a consolation that God would watch over him and forgive him. "It must be moldering somewhere in the forest, along with my hopes for evangelism," he thought. "Perhaps I had better start getting used to living without it."

Beyond the Covenant

Captain Roy Morrison swayed with the corkscrew rhythm of the seas as he made his way towards the bow of the freighter *Mary Foster*, hanging onto the guideline that stretched toward the forecastle. As the passage of a roller pitched the ship up to its crest, he looked northward to the South African coast for the Cape Agulhas light, but saw only a dim confusion of cloud and spray. Too late to turn back now, he thought. At the end of the line he caught at the handle of the hatchway and let himself into the warm, bright refuge of the crew's quarters. But he could smell the rot as soon as he got inside. Billy Barney, the first mate, was in one of the rooms with Coelho. He had cleared it out when the first symptoms appeared and gone inside with his medical kit. Morrison had promised to recommend Barney for his own command if he came out alive. He rapped two short knocks on the door of the room.

"Still here, Captain. No change in the patient. Not for the better anyway. Fever's the same. He bleeds from the ears a little."

"Still got food?"

"Plenty. But you can have someone slip in another pint of rum. It can do double duty because I'm almost out of carbolic."

"Right." Morrison paused, not knowing what to say. "Carry on."

As he turned he saw the chief engineer Petersen in the corridor behind him, puffing on a stubby pipe. The engineer said nothing and peered at him through a slight cloud of smoke.

"Well," said Morrison. "Anything to report?"

Petersen slowly drew the pipe from his teeth and replied, "She's holding her speed pretty well, sir. Of course if we turned..."

"Can we make Colombo?"

"Aye, sir, Colombo and probably Calcutta, too, unless this storm lasts more than four days."

"Then maintain speed," said Morrison, and shoved past the engineer to head back to the bridge.

Petersen walked past the quarantine cabin and into the crowded space beyond, where the next watch was getting ready to go on duty. A sailor named Bellows accosted him, "Hey, Fishy, was that the skipper you were talking to out there?"

"It was," answered Petersen, "Though I hadn't intended to pass the time of day with him."

Bellows drew the Dane closer and looked over his shoulder as though he expected someone to be spying at the door. "Look here, did he go in to see poor Coelho, or did he just knock at the door?"

"Just knocked," said Petersen, poking at the bowl of his pipe, "As usual."

"Old Cappy Ryan would never have let a sailor go deadly sick on board. Die on board and get dumped in the sea."

"That Morrison's no fit man to sail with." The interjection came from an older man with sideburns who had been listening along with the rest of the watch.

"Really, Porter," said the skeptical Petersen. "And what would Ryan have done?"

"Put into Durban. Or Lorenço Marquez, an Allied harbor, or a neutral one, if he was afraid of mines. Any port with a decent doctor ashore. Ryan was a sailor's sailor and never would have let a crewman down." Porter puffed out his chest at the proud memory of the *Mary Foster's* former master.

"Aye, but it's war now," ventured Bellows. "That cargo of tanks and trucks we took on in Cape Town is under a timed contract for the army in India. I suppose we should do our patriotic duty to get it there."

"Hah!" snorted a clean-shaven fellow in his twenties. "That contract increases the shipper's profit with every day we shave from the delivery. And you can bet Morrison's in for a share of that. A share the forecastle will never see."

"Calm down, Red," chimed in several voices from the watch. "You'd stay under way with a crew full of corpses if you could get into Odessa."

A thin, nervous laugh spread through the cabin, with even Red taking part to relieve the pent-up pressure. Worry about the strange disease that Coelho had brought aboard in Cape Town. Worry about the gale that was blowing in their face. Worry about the unfamiliar captain who had been sent to take over their ship only two months earlier. Worry about the unknown out beyond the storm, on the waves and beneath them.

Petersen calmly lit up his pipe again and pronounced, "Red may be right. The captain seems hell-bent on unloading his cargo on time. At least he knows what he wants. Still, I am going to talk to Cunningham to see if he can convince Morrison into heading for Durban. The Captain would never go to a neutral Portuguese port, where a U-boat could pin him in for the rest of the war."

The watch, swathed in slickers and sou'westers followed him out the hatch into the screaming wind and manned their posts.

Back on the bridge, Morrison shook the seawater off his outer clothes and hung them on pegs. He used the new electric communicator to call the forecastle and spoke to one of the past watch just turning back in, ordering the sailor to slip a bottle of rum through the door to Barney. The electric communicators had been installed to deal with the din of battle. For service in this new war, *Mary Foster* had been fitted with a four-inch cannon and an antiaircraft Bofors gun. When they were firing no normal human voice could be heard. But the communicator served equally well over a Roaring Forties gale. Morrison turned to watch his Second Mate Cunningham at the wheel. The young officer's eyes were riveted to the compass binnacle as he struggled to keep the bow as far into the wind as the course would permit. Morrison cast a cursory glance at the gauges before telling Cunningham that he was taking an hour's rest. The captain's cabin offered a welcome nest, even if it pitched crazily as the rollers struck and ran the length of the hull. A picture of a vine-covered cottage overlooking the Bristol Channel hung on the bulkhead, alongside framed certificates tracing Morrison's career as a merchant marine officer. Secured within the little desk was a book with all his recommendations, each one mentioning his punctuality and dependability. When Roy Morrison entered into an agreement to deliver his cargo at a certain time and place, that was paramount.

Really should have taken medical training, too, thought the captain. Bad luck to have a fever on board this first trip into the Indian Ocean. What could it be? Plague? Dengue? Marsh fever? As if the parasites were not enough, Africa was swarming with every imaginable form of fever and bloody flux! Good thing Barney was on board with a little bush-doctor experience and enough ambition to play nursemaid to that wretch Coelho. Or more likely undertaker. Morrison had seen the livid patches and pustules on the seaman's skin and the blood oozing from his ears and eyes. He was sure Coelho wouldn't last another night, not long enough to make Durban. And if they did, he might die just as the doctor was coming on board to quarantine the *Mary Foster* for a month or more. If Morrison was to continue to collect testimonials to his seamanship, he didn't need forced time ashore. Especially if he continued to chase that secret little dream of his, a true naval command. Officer casualties had already been high and in this part of the world, it was not unheard of for an exceptional master to be offered service on a Royal Navy ship. Perhaps only an oiler or transport, but he would gladly accept any old hulk that flew a naval pennant overhead. He fell asleep dreaming of being piped aboard and reviewing a crew in immaculate uniforms.

    Cunningham's forearms were just getting tired from his unending struggle with the wheel when Petersen came onto the bridge. The wrinkled Dane nodded at the second mate and offered, "I'd be willing to stand a while at the wheel if you'd like to break for a cup of tea."
    "Gladly! How are things below?"
    "Oh, she strains a bit in this sort of gale, but we're good for at least another week before we have to give the engines a once-over."
    "That isn't what I meant."
    "The human part of the ship is not so easy to keep oiled," responded the engineer.

Cunningham cupped his hands around a mug of strong dark tea that had been steeping under a gray cozy for hours. He looked cautiously at the impassive Petersen, who seemed to be able to draw on his pipe without any audible breathing. "You've been at sea a lot longer than me. How bad is it? How much more will the crew take before they break loose?"

"They're good boys and they know their profession," Petersen nodded. "But we were all attached to Ryan. He made each one of us know we were men, worthwhile in our own right. I suppose we all blame Morrison a bit for taking Ryan's command. It wasn't natural that the old captain should go on half-pay ashore at his age and in the middle of a war. Where do you stand?"

The question took Cunningham aback. Though he had come aboard at the same time as Morrison, he had never known the man before he stepped on the *Mary Foster* and he resented the fact that many crewmen considered him a minion of the new captain. "I stand where I have to stand. As an officer, there's no question of my opposing a skipper of sound mind and body. You must understand that, Petersen, you're more than a common stoker yourself."

Petersen ignored the compliment and stared at Cunningham with intense eyes. "Then, you'd better do something while you still have a choice. You can talk to Morrison. Tell him how the men feel. Tell him about the risks of a two thousand mile cruise past the U-boats with an uncooperative crew. And what if he does get the damned trucks to Calcutta before the deadline? Nothing changes then. Not with the boys in the forecastle. It can only get worse."

"What alternative do we have?"

"Durban is closer than Mozambique. It's protected by planes and patrol boats. No chance of being blockaded there, like in a neutral port. True, we'll have the weather more amidships, at least for a while. But we can be there in less than eight hours, unload Coelho's carcass, swab out and get a clean bill of health, and miss a good part of the storm to boot. We'll raise Colombo a lot faster at ten knots than at five. No net loss."

Cunningham had already figured out most of the pro's and con's himself during his hours at the wheel, but he was nevertheless impressed by the Dane's concise grip of the situation. He had never expected this kind of sharp thinking from a forecastle philosopher. On the other hand, with so much intelligence,

Petersen would be a dangerous antagonist if it came to breaking out the new side arms against a mutinous crew. "If I were to do my best with the captain..." Cunningham paused, "Would you promise to keep the crew in line?"

"The question is : could I keep that promise?"

"I'd be sticking my neck out to argue with a senior officer on my third assignment. I could be blacklisted in every port east of Suez. I want to get something for my trouble."

"What about your conscience?" Petersen intoned. "Don't you care about Coelho? Maybe you think officers float around on little antiseptic clouds, but had you stepped into a wrong bit of dust and germs, that could be you in there with Billy."

"I took an oath. A binding agreement to obey orders and serve."

"Is the oath more important than the man that makes it?"

Cunningham gulped down the rest of his syrupy tea and stepped to the wheel. "I'd better take over again, now," he said. He really needed time to think out what Petersen had suggested. "Listen, Fishy, don't tell the men too much about our little exchange. I don't say yes and I don't say no."

"You can't fret forever," growled Petersen. "I'll be back in an hour."

Within minutes, members of the new watch returned from their on-deck errands and took over the wheel. Cunningham made his way along the precarious guideline toward the forecastle and stopped outside the quarantine cabin. He coughed, then knocked, and was answered by a weary Billy Barney, "Yes, what is it?"

Since the door didn't open, the second mate reluctantly came closer and spoke louder. "It's me, Cunningham, how's he doing, Billy?"

"Won't die," Billy shot back, "But he's not alive by very much either. Tough little bugger, I suppose. If he ever gets out of this, he'll think he's indestructible."

"Billy, listen, the men are pretty hard against Morrison."

"I can imagine. One reason I'm not sad to be in here instead of out there with you. I don't imagine they'll come storming in to take it out on me."

"You knew Morrison before. Can I appeal to him? Is he likely to put into port if I convince him of the danger?"

Barney thought a long moment. "Morrison's like granite. He very seldom changes his opinion on anything. He has the confidence of the owners. They hand-picked him to replace Ryan because they thought the old man was going soft and costing them dividends."

Cunningham's hopes were fading. "What if I held the owners up against him? Wouldn't he be afraid it might change their minds if the crew made trouble?"

"He has an iron-clad contract," Barney blurted out. "First of its kind. Full salary for six years even if he's ashore. Engraved in stone by God the Father himself. You'd best make up your mind to stand behind him. Or find a nice quiet place for the storm to blow over and hope he doesn't survive."

Cunningham started to walk back to the hatchway and turned again. "Will you come out and help? Will you raise a pistol against our own crew?"

"Don't think so. You see, I can seal this cabin pretty well. May not need to, though. I'm starting to feel not so well myself. Think I'll lie down. Don't bother sending in another nursemaid." There was a silence that seemed very long. "It may be I've chosen badly."

Petersen met Cunningham on the way up to the bridge. "The men in the engine room have started to set aside tools and axes. Hidden under a tarp here and a box there. But close at hand. You don't have long. Make it good." Then he disappeared down the corridor.

Cunningham went to the captain's cabin and knocked until he woke up Morrison. Bleary-eyed, the skipper opened the door and once he recognized his second mate, he waved the young man into his quarters.

"What's the cause of all this commotion?"

"Sir, I have to report that the first mate is becoming ill and I respectfully request that we put into the port of Durban with all possible speed."

"Hmm. Well rehearsed. Surely you didn't come up with that all by yourself. I smell a Dane behind it."

"Sir, some of the men have talked with me. They don't want to challenge you, sir, but this just doesn't seem right... to them. "

"And what about you?"

"Personally, sir, I, I... well, with two crewmen sick..."

"Two?"

"Barney, as well. And the others on the brink of disorder. I think the only prudent thing is to put into Durban."

"Or become the victims of mutineers?"

"Er, yes, so it would appear, sir."

"I'm not worried!" declared Morrison.

"But the ship, sir, as officers, we are responsible...."

"Perhaps I know something you don't." When Cunningham could only stare quizzically back, Morrison suddenly grabbed a set of keys and lurched down the corridor, stopping at the first mate's usual cabin. He unlocked the hatch and invited his second mate to have a look. Inside were a half dozen Royal Marines with submachine guns lounging around the compartment in various attitudes of half-sleep.

When Cunningham looked incredulously back at Morrison, the captain was lighting a cigarette in a very self-confident manner. "You see, these fellows were down guarding the munitions in the holds, but with the storm I suggested they spend the night up here. Especially since the first mate was otherwise occupied. Are you still worried about a few grease monkeys armed with wrenches?"

"No, sir," blurted Cunningham. "But that doesn't change the fate of the men who are ill. Don't you care about them? Leaving Barney sealed up in that plague cabin like a tomb just about broke my heart. Is it so great a delay just to see them into safe hands or into a decent grave?"

Morrison looked more serious. "This is war. Many men will die, but we can't let ourselves go all to pieces with the first sign of bloodshed. These men signed on to this ship promising to give all in return for their wages. The pledge will be honored in full. I will see to it. I promised to get these munitions to Calcutta in time for them to be used by the Indian Army. That promise will be honored in full. Need I remind you of your own engagements?"

"I know I promised to obey and I will. But you are captain, sir," objected Cunningham. "Look, everyone acknowledges that you are master of this ship. While we are at sea, no one, not even the owners can countermand you or call you into question. And these men ask nothing more than the chance to serve you with some respect. What in God's name is to stop you from showing a little judgment, a little mercy, a little consideration for those two up in the forecastle?"

"I am. I hold myself to judgment. I am also able to stop myself from doing anything so foolish. Because it is not what I have promised to do. Now go explain to Petersen what the situation is. Tell him about the Marines. Can't keep that surprise forever, anyway."

Cunningham descended stairways and ladders down into the engineer's realm. A place of percussion and vibration, where enormous forces were pressed into a discipline of thermodynamics and mechanical precision and channeled into the whirling blades that invisibly propelled the *Mary Foster* through the ice-cold seas. Down in that humid and strange-smelling forest of cams and pipes and valves, Cunningham found the Dane, as imperturbable as ever, clenching his extinguished pipe in his teeth and waiting. He seemed to know the bad news before the mate could open his mouth.

Cunningham made profuse apologies. Then he told the engineer about the Marines.

"Don't worry, lad," consoled the wizened sailor, "You've tried your best. Made your plea for humanity and it failed. After all, it wasn't in the contract. Somehow, that kind of thing never is. Time now to think of the rest of the crew that are still alive."

Suddenly a group of seamen appeared at the foot of the stairs, looking like a Viking raiding party. Red and Bellows carried axes from the fire stations, Porter hefted an enormous pipe wrench, and Cho Sing, the cook, held his Chinese cleaver. Some of the others had nothing more than folding knives or marlinspikes. Petersen could not help chuckling when he saw them and muttered to Cunningham, "As the novels would say, a lubberly lot of scoundrels." The Dane went over to the little force and told them it was no good, the boss had a detachment of heavily armed Marines aft, ready to mow them down, and they'd best behave themselves until they got to Calcutta. Cunningham was surprised by the way Petersen closed his little speech.

"....and as for me, I'm going to turn myself over to Captain Morrison as the ringleader of this little Kaffeeklatsch and sit for a while in the brig. In any case, he would have me arrested if I did not. That should keep him happy for the rest of the trip."

Petersen's surrender, pronounced in such a magnanimous way, did not fail to elicit claps on the back and a few tears from his fellow crewmen. As calculated, it completely disarmed them. Petersen followed Cunningham back up the ladders to the bridge. "I do have one last idea and plan to use that as a bargaining chip with the captain. Since he can't resist the power of a covenant, perhaps I can still find one last way to get Coelho and Barney some medical help."

"What do you have in mind?"

"Maybe a way to save something without giving up the word of the law. A move I learned from an old herring fisherman back home. The trick will be to make him believe he thought of it himself. But then, he is so vain, perhaps that will not be such a trick after all."

"What can I do for you, Petersen?" asked the mate, feeling guilty that he would survive this nasty business while the engineer was to be brought up on charges in Colombo or Calcutta. "Can I talk to a consul for you? Is there anyone you know?"

Petersen answered slowly. "You know, there's not much of Denmark left any more, right now. This ship is the only real home I have. Still, it's better than staying behind in occupation with no choices left at all. Don't worry about me. I dare say I know enough about machines to draw some pretty easy time in the clink."

When they reached the bridge, the Dane motioned for Cunningham to stay behind and he went to confront Morrison alone. A few minutes later, he emerged with a smile on his face and nodded to the mate as a Marine ushered him aft towards the damp little compartment that served as brig and cable locker on the *Mary Foster*. Beaming, Morrison hurried forward, almost bumping into Cunningham.

"Ah, there you are. Up to the radio shack and send out a message to any allied shipping inbound toward South Africa. Tell them we seek a ship's doctor to see to two sick men."

He said it as though it were his own idea.

A half-hour later, Cunningham knocked on the door of the captain's cabin. "I managed to raise a Dutchman out of Batavia bound for Cape Town. *Hoogenboom's* got a surgeon on board and can rendezvous with us in about four hours. He offered to bring them to Durban."

"So you see, Cunningham, I was right. If everyone holds up his own end of the agreement, everything comes out right."

"Yes sir. Still, lucky the Dutch freighter was willing to care for a couple of helpless devils." He could not prevent himself from adding, as he went out the door, "Not even their own people, either."

Morrison took a second to get the point of the remark, then considered calling the mate back, but instead lit a cigarette and settled down with a copy of Royal Navy regulations. As night was falling, he lit an extra light in his cabin. Might be dealing with new rules very soon, he thought.

The rays of light went out the porthole and penetrated into the murky mixture of sea and air that cascaded around the ship. They split up and scattered and spread over the gray-green water and some entered a metal tube and reflected in two mirrors before emerging in the periscope sights of U-123. Oberleutnant Schilling recorded the bearing and turned to his commander. "Same course, sir. What orders?"

Kapitänleutnant Ballauf looked him in the eye and shot back, "What would your orders be if you were in command?"

"Well," Schilling paused, "At this point in the conflict, we should not waste our torpedoes. We are far from our re-supply point. But the seas right now do not permit an attack with the deck gun." Ballauf was nodding slowly to encourage the young submariner, but he threw up his hands when his protégé concluded, "So we should wait a few hours and then surface and open fire with the cannon."

"Kvatsch!" shouted Ballauf. "Who knows whether the seas will be calmer then? And have you forgotten the message we intercepted about their meeting with the Dutchman? Do you suppose that even a Hollander will just stand around while you shell the English ship, waiting for its turn? You have to learn to be creative with any situation."

Ballauf turned to his navigator. "Have you calculated the course to the rendezvous point with *Hoogenboom*?"

"Yes captain. All ready. All in order."

"So now," Ballauf said to Schilling, "You know what to do."

Schilling went to the communicator and ordered the forward torpedo tubes to load one. Then he looked to his captain, who was frowning.

"We don't have time to play around, Lieutnant!" He held up two fingers.

Schilling added a second torpedo to the order and prepared the periscope to sight the launch. One! Two! Two obedient metal fish, very heavy with doom. Hot, straight, and normal. *Mary Foster* broke in two from the force of explosions in the cargo holds and the two ends of the ship sank instantly, quelling the fevers and ambitions of all aboard, ending all confinements and all anticipation. Loosening all bonds.

Aboard U-123 Schilling and his captain headed back to their tiny compartments to fill out the reports contractually required of all German Navy officers. On the threshold of his cabin, Schilling whispered to Ballauf, "Thanks for not scolding me in front of the men."

Ballauf smiled benevolently. "I always take care of my crew."

The Sheepskin Jacket

Marty's 4 by 4 was bucking like a honky-tonk mechanical bull as it followed the dirt road around Suspicion Mountain. The dogs in the back couldn't settle down and kept scrambling back and forth, excited by the scents of autumn game on the wind.

"In a way, I suppose I should be glad we won't have to come up here anymore. It will save me a fortune on realignments."

"I'm sure Uncle Bill wanted us to continue to spend every summer and fall up at the cabin," answered Steve. "But I just want one more good shot at those pheasants up there and then I'm ready to bail. I should get a half million easy for the place, judging by the development that's going in around Grand Junction. That will set me up fine for a long time. A half million will buy a lot time in a hot tub and plenty of fine Chardonnay."

"Still, I'll miss the serenity of the place. There's something about that long, unbroken view of the valley. It just keeps on stretching west and makes me feel I'm at the edge of the world. Some place trouble hasn't found yet."

"I bring my troubles wherever I go, I suppose. But a half million is going to go a long way to dissolving some of them. For one thing I can get Anna and her alimony and her child support off my back for a while."

"I would have thought that a woman like her would have found somebody by now. No offense, mind you," Marty added hastily, "but you have to admit she kept her figure uncommonly well after having that baby and, well, some guys might not be bothered as much by her nagging."

"They'd have to work mighty late hours not to get bothered by that," huffed Steve. "She ruined too many good times for me."

The cabin came into view around the bend, still shuttered from last spring, when the cousins had sealed it up after Bill's funeral. Leaves and pinecones littered the little porch, yet the place looked intact. No visible holes betrayed the snooping of bears or raccoons. They grabbed bags and coolers full of groceries and headed inside, quickly opening all the windows to let out the stale air. As Marty reset the fridge to its proper setting and started to stack perishables inside, Steve and the dogs headed for the door.

"Listen, you don't mind taking care of that for now, do you? The weather is perfect to go bag a couple of birds."

"Suit yourself," shrugged Marty, "Just don't go shooting anywhere down near the stream. I'm going down and see if I can find a trout or two as soon as I secure this stuff."

Without the nervous dogs under foot to trip him up, Marty was surprised that the household tasks took less time than he had anticipated. As he carried his tackle down to the stream, he heard the report of Steve's shotgun echoing over the hill. He thought back to *The Compleat Angler* and the way Isaak Walton had drawn a distinction between hunters and fishermen. It certainly held true for him and his cousin. "Poor Venator," he mused to himself, "Steve will never be able to be at peace with the land as I can be. Old Isaak was right. Piscator feels more in step with nature. He must become like nature if he wants to harvest it." He put a fall fly on the end of his line and cast into a pool below him that might be deep enough to harbor a late season rainbow.

When he returned to the cabin a couple of hours later, he was surprised to find Steve already there, cursing and opening all the closets and drawers. "Damn, damn, double damn!" he fumed. "I got up on that rock wall near the old pasture looking to see where a bird had fallen. A nice big cock pheasant I definitely winged. The dogs had taken off after it, but I couldn't see where they were in the brush. Anyway, no sooner had I climbed up there to look then some of the rocks gave way and pitched me down into a tangle of old barbed wire."

"Did you cut yourself? I'll get the medical kit."

"No, I hardly got a scratch, but look what it did to my new microfibre shooting jacket!" The expensive cloth looked like a bobcat had used it to sharpen its claws.

"Steve, I don't think you're going to be able to sew that back together yourself."

"Nuts. I can't go out shooting with just a flannel shirt. Where am I going to keep my shells? Besides, it looks like it's fixing to start a good two-day blow and I'll freeze my butt off."

Marty thought for a minute. "Didn't Uncle Bill keep an old sheepskin jacket up here someplace? It seems to me it had deep pockets that would hold at least a dozen rounds apiece. He used to carry his books or his camera in them when he went out to walk. Sometimes a sandwich and a flask of something to drink. Where could it be? I don't remember us throwing it away."

"You think that old relic is still here? It was probably finished off by the moths a long time ago," Steve objected, as he looked skeptically into a closet.

"Maybe it's in one of those chests up in the attic?"

They clambered up the old ladder, pushed open the trap door, and found the attic remarkably free of dust and spiders. It smelled of the tufts of herbs that Bill had told them he hung in the corners to keep out unwanted visitors. Fortunately the chests, like the rest of the cabin, were unlocked. They found the sheepskin jacket in the second one they tried. It was intact, wrapped in plastic with a bag of desiccant and some more herbs. Pretty worn around the collar, and one big metal button didn't match any of the others, but otherwise it seemed serviceable.

"I don't know," grumbled Steve. "This thing is ancient. Couldn't I wear one of your jackets?" Marty noticed that he held the garment at arm's length, as if to avoid contact. Yet he could smell no mustiness from where he was standing, and he wondered what made Steve so squeamish about putting the jacket to good use. It looked like a perfect fit.

"You know they'd be too tight in the shoulders, especially the way you thrash around when you're shooting. This one will do fine for the time being. It's probably warmer than that thing you picked up at the mall, anyway."

Steve grabbed it and shook it out and reluctantly went back down the ladder into the main room of the cabin. He was not convinced. He had been eager to find a replacement for the ruined microfiber masterpiece, but all of a sudden he had developed an odd feeling about this sheepskin hand-me-down. Perhaps something associated with his old uncle or their childhood visits to the place. He couldn't quite put his finger on it and the more he pondered it, the more confused he felt. Whatever it was, it couldn't be logical.

Marty, the Piscator, got up long before Steve the next morning, reasoning that his best chance of landing a trout was in the dim light of dawn when the fish might be hungry. He was not wrong. When he got back, he found Steve in the kitchen sipping a mug of coffee, and he proudly opened up his creel. "Look at those beauties! Fresh fillets tonight, at least for the human beings. All others," he added, looking at the dogs, "will have to make do with Alpo."

"Don't be too sure. I'm going back up and find that pheasant I shot, if a cougar hasn't already taken it away. Maybe get a few more. Be prepared to pop those in the freezer if I get my way!"

"No way. You'll want to hang those birds for a day, anyhow. If they decide to let you execute them."

"No if's, and's, or but's about it."

"I see you decided to wear that sheepskin."

Steve squirmed a little in it. "It feels weird. It's not tight in the armpits, but something is just not right. Maybe I need to break it in a little."

"Well, good luck," said Marty. "As for me, my morning's work is done, and I left a nice bottle of wine down in the well to cool. It should be perfect right now."

As he walked out through the old pasture where Bill used to keep some sheep years ago, Steve remembered what they looked like as they grazed and could almost hear them bleat. That old black ram called Moses, he said to himself, he always wanted to be the boss of the flock. Bill said he wouldn't be surprised to wake up some day and find he'd led all the ewes away in search of the Promised Land.

"Why do you suppose he doesn't," little Steve had asked him one day.

"Because the Promised Land is right here. Unlike the other Moses, this one got to enjoy the pastures of Canaan."

Old Uncle Bill certainly had some strange ideas about religion. Steve never could remember him having crossed the threshold of a church, but he was always spouting off about God. I guess this jacket is haunted, he thought. It's giving me flashbacks of the past.

He was more careful than yesterday when he crossed the crumbling old stone wall, and with the help of his dogs he soon found the body of the pheasant in fine shape in the branches of a shrub. He was about to stuff it in the game bag, but he stopped and carefully examined its head, fascinated by the reds and purples that still flashed in its feathers. No wonder the Indians made feather headdresses! Of course they didn't have pheasants. These plumes seemed to have a life of their own that survived the hunter. There was still a Bird Spirit in there somewhere, blinking at him with an unseen eye. He held out the wing, counted the flight feathers, preened out the tail, touched the claws and the beak. When he finally did put it into the bag, he whistled a little tune and tried to get back in the shooting mood. But as he continued across the hills a stinging wind seemed always to be in his face. He didn't see another bird for hours. On the way back, the game sack seemed heavy on his back. I must be out of shape, he thought.

The cousins ate the trout that night, sautéed in butter with some shallots and rice.

The next morning when Marty came back to the cabin after his fly-fishing, he was less sanguine. "Just a couple of nibbles this morning. If you don't get any more pheasant, I guess it's pasta this evening." When Steve didn't answer immediately he looked at him more attentively. "Hey, where's your shotgun?"

"Well, I just don't think I want to shoot today. This jacket still doesn't fit just right. Maybe I twisted my shoulder a little when I fell off that wall."

"Better give it a rest, then. Need a novel to while away some time?"

"No, I think I'm just going to walk out again today and look around."

Steve had to admit that the sheepskin was nice and warm for an autumn morning. Without the game bag, he felt himself stepping out into a lively march. The dogs came and went as they wished, sometimes exploring far up into the rockfalls or down towards the stream's winding bed, then rushing dementedly back to prance around, as though they could communicate to him the excitement of whatever scents they had encountered. Unconsciously, Steve wandered farther up the slopes than he had ever gone, into terrain unsuitable for hunting birds. He stopped in odd places, not because there was something really peculiar to see or because he was tired, but simply because something told him to stop and look. He noticed for the first time that there were some big hawks in the valley and that they must be his rivals for the pheasants in the tall grass. It was nearly nightfall when he finally came back in view of the house. Marty had made spaghetti with marinara sauce and they ate it with relish. That night Steve dreamed of hawks, soaring on the invisible currents of wind rising off the mountains.

Marty was surprised the next day that Steve had arisen before him and breakfasted on bagels and coffee before the sun was really up above the ridges. "Venator develops new ways. Or perhaps not." The trout seemed unconcerned that it was Sunday. He filled his creel before two in the afternoon. Steve had not come back for lunch. A quick examination of the fridge revealed that he had opened some luncheon meat to make sandwiches and the bottle of white wine was almost empty. "He must have found Uncle Bill's old flask and packed himself a meal."

Indeed, the lunch had fit easily into the pocket of the old sheepskin jacket and the flask stayed cool and fresh until he stopped to lunch on a high col looking over into the next valley. After lunch he fell asleep in the sun and didn't wake until the dogs swarmed, slurping all over him, wanting to start the return trip. On the way back he found a big rose quartz crystal that he put in one pocket, then further on, the skull of a badger, bleached by the wind and weather. I could just about fit the whole badger in there with it, he joked to himself. A new feeling. "Maybe I've been too serious."

When he got back to the cabin, he was surprised to find Marty packing up parcels and shuttering the windows. He had forgotten it was Sunday evening and they were returning to the city, to their jobs. For a second, he realized he was glad he had forgotten.

"Take off that old rag and I'll stick it back up in the attic. We need to hit the road by six."

"No," Steve said, pausing. "I'll just hang it here in the closet where it won't get wrinkled."

"That's where it always belonged," remarked Marty. "But if you unload the place this week, are you going to leave it there for the new owners? Chances are they won't even look inside before they bulldoze this place."

"If I sell, if I decide to sell, I'll make sure to come get it first. I don't think I'll sell it that soon. Maybe I should let it appreciate a little. I'll just leave the sheepskin jacket right here."

Headed back down the winding mountain road, with the headlights already piercing into the shadows that were gathering under the evergreens, Marty said, "I guess you won't miss this ride anymore. But then, I forgot, you said you'd be coming back up. So when do you want me to come pick you up?"

"Next weekend is my weekend with Amanda," Steve explained, looking out the window into the forest. "She's only five, but I found a place up there where there are a whole lot of ground squirrels. I bet she'll get a kick out of watching them. Maybe we can even feed them some peanuts. I think I'll try bringing her up here. Next time, cuz'," he said, turning to Marty, "I'll pick you up."

Middle Management

Gabi opened the lab door and peered in. Izzy was in his normal seat in front of the batrachian experiment, listening to his beloved frogs through the earphones. Even without the electronics, Gabi could hear their harmonic chirping through the enclosures.

She walked up to her rapt fellow researcher and tapped him on the shoulder. He was so accustomed to her presence, to her return at this precise hour, that he merely smiled vaguely in her direction and waved his hand without breaking his focus on the batrachians.

It was not until Mike returned from the avian compound that Izzy lifted off his earphones and triumphantly exclaimed, "Did you ever hear such beautiful music in your life?

They've organized their calls into chords, into chords! I can't wait to tell the Boss. Where is he, anyway?"

Mike spoke up and explained, "I passed him on the way back from the aviary. He was headed down to the mammalian experiment and he didn't look very happy." The strapping ornithologist walked over to Gabi and gave her a lingering look that was returned in kind.

Izzy paid little attention because he had known for some time that they had become intimate. "I'm hoping he will finally close down that primate thing."

"It hasn't been going at all well, that's true," noted Gabi. "But what interest do you have in it?"

"Protein. That's a lot of animal protein that should not go to waste. Just think what my batrachians could do with that kind of protein source! They'll be creating symphonies in no time."

"But what if the Boss doesn't agree? After all, we can't go around closing down operations just to feed to your frogs. Why did you design them to be carnivorous, anyway? The Boss warned you about that."

"Don't be silly, Gabi. There's no reason to throw away perfectly good biomass. What do you think, Mike?"

"I agree with Gabi. It seems a little bit ghoulish to be making those mammalians into a menu for your subjects."

Izzy pouted. "So why don't you modify your eagles and falcons into herbivores if you're so keen on achieving ecological balance?"

"You can't make that comparison,"? retorted Mike. "There's got to be priorities for higher order avian species."

"You two should have followed my lead," said Gabi. "My cephalopods are omnivorous. When there are no fish available, they convert to feeding on algae. Very sensible."

"But Gabi, dear, that's fine for sea creatures," answered Mike. "But how can you expect big birds to feed on vegetation? Eagles and hawks are at the top of the food chain. We can't let them start gobbling down spruce trees or it would put everything in their environment topsy-turvy. The smaller species would soon starve."

"That's why the sea is such an advantage," Gabi said, shaking her blonde locks. "Liquidity, freedom of exchange between different levels."

Izzy chimed in. "That's where I have you both beaten! My amphibians can have the best of both worlds. Of course, they can't fly yet. But they already sing and communicate better than your birds ever could, Mike. And Gabi, all your octopi can do is primitive touch communication and color changing. I submit that my creatures are the highest achievement of this lab." He pushed back his glasses as if to make a point.

Gabi shrugged her shoulders in her delightfully ingenuous way. "Well, I don't see how we can resolve this argument."

A suave voice cut in from behind them. "I can. You're all a crew of idiots and all your animals belong in the trash bin."

Unbeknownst to the trio, a fourth scientist in a spotless lab coat had silently entered the room during their conversation.

Izzy eyed him suspiciously. "Ah, the great philosopher is back. Where have you been, Nick, while we were working?"

"You call that work, you four-eyed geek? Those frogs of yours are on the edge of extinction. You want the mammal protein because you still haven't got their metabolism properly engineered. I offered to give you the benefit of my genetic knowledge, but you have floundered around, screwing up the math, letting all sorts of dangerous recessive traits develop, while you rhapsodize over their stupid chants."

Izzy blushed. He did not know which made him more upset, the personal insults or the truth of Nick's assessment of his beloved batrachians. With his usual incisiveness and acid wit, Nick had bored straight to the weakness of Izzy's project. He slouched back over his desk and tried to work once again on the biochemistry that had been puzzling him.

With Izzy cringing in defeat, Nick made his way over to Gabi's table. "Maybe you should be the one I help. I think you've already had enough tips about those squids to owe me a little something."

Gabi looked up apprehensively. "I really am grateful for your help. But we are all a team, aren't we? Why does everything seem to have a price for you?"

Nick leered at her. "Because I'm the one who controls the marketplace."

Mike came over and deliberately moved his muscular body between Nick and Gabi. "Haven't you forgotten about the Boss?" he asked. "After all, you're only assistant director."

"Do you see the Boss now?" ranted Nick, flinging his arms in a circle to indicate the entire lab. "Do you ever see him around here much? He's clueless these days. He literally doesn't know what's happening with the projects. I think he's up there in his office snoozing most of the day."

I don't know, Nick. It's true he hasn't been in much. But I don't think he ever sleeps. Every time I tell him something about the avians, he already seems to know."

"That's because your work is so simple-minded it doesn't exactly require a great intellect to take it all in. It's the right thing for someone with a second-rate degree, though. You couldn't begin to manage the marine project, for instance. You're only good for swabbing out cages."

Mike pursed his lips and made a movement toward Nick, but Gabi reached out and put a hand on his shoulder to hold him back, shaking her head to remind him it was not wise to confront this arrogant superior.

"That's right," chortled Nick. "You know the score, honey. I'll be number one around here before long and only those who know their places will have any hope of staying on." He sidled around to Gabi and reached out to caress her neck. "And you know your place, don't you, Gabi? Under me!"

She brushed away his hand as though it were covered with slime, rose and took a couple of steps away.

Nick's leer had instantly turned into a glare of hatred. "Bitch!" he sneered, curling his lip. "Goddamn whore! You're more slippery than anything over in Izzy's little swamp. Think you're too sophisticated for me? I'll have you scrubbing out test tubes back in no time if I want to. And I want to. Hell, I'll have you handling contagious stuff at some hospital in the slums."

Mike moved menacingly close to Nick and lowered his voice. "Lay off her, now Nick. Nobody here wants to cause trouble for you, but I won't let you bully her."

Nick answered Mike's threat with mocking laughter. "Hah! The great hero comes to the rescue! Gabi, I can't believe that instead of me, you'll go down with the half-wit of Notre Dame, here."

Mike's fist came flying and landed square on Nick's jaw. It seemed enough to knock him into the next room, but to everyone's surprise, Nick merely turned his head back slowly and felt the reddened spot where the punch had landed. It looked as though an insect had had the impudence to sting him and he was curious about the effect. He looked up at Mike and hissed, "You've sealed your fate, now, stupid. In the monthly report I'm going to let you have it. I've been saving up a few things. And just to show you how it's done, when you're gone, I think I'll take over the avians myself and have a little fun. I've got a few recombinant strains I've been working on and it will be interesting to see how virulent they are. Interesting to see the effects on those birds when they can't get off the ground."

Mike became visibly scared, not so much for himself as for the eagles and falcons he had come to regard almost as pets, even though they were completely adapted in a wild habitat. He realized his strength could not protect them. Perhaps not Gabi either, if it came to that. Nick seemed to have anticipated any reaction anyone might make.

Izzy, who had been meekly watching the confrontation, cleared his throat and tried to change the subject. "Nick, is the Boss going to close down the mammalian project? Are you going to recommend it?"

Nick's eyes refocused and a strange smile came over his face. "No, I don't think it's time just yet. We haven't closed down an experiment in a long time."

"Not since the the Boss terminated the reptile experiment," said Izzy, who immediately regretted he'd mentioned it. The reptiles had been Nick's domain and he had been furious when, for some reason no one could readily understand, the Boss had ordered it ended and reassigned Nick to general administrative duties.

"Yes, I know what you're thinking, four-eyes!" said Nick. "Those lizards meant a lot to me and showed how much I could do. They were splendid, and it was a waste to let them go."

"Though I hate to admit it," conceded Mike, "I couldn't help but admire their strength and toughness. They were amazingly aggressive. Almost unstoppable."

"Yeah. Even an oaf like you could see that much. But they were so much more. More than any of you could grasp. Or him. It showed how much he was already slipping when he took away my creatures. And look what we've got instead. A bunch of failures."

"They wouldn't have failed if you had devoted some of your superior intelligence to solving their problems," observed Gabi.

"You're right about that. And that's why I've been doing a little free-lancing with the apes down at the mammalian project. That's why he's down there now, trying to figure out what went wrong. He thinks the breeding protocols are all screwed up and the mating imprints aren't working. As I said, he doesn't have a clue. I'll soon show that what I did with the reptiles was just a taste of what I can achieve."

The three colleagues were alarmed by this revelation and burst into objections.

"How could you tamper with that project? What did you do? It's a delicate experiment in environmental ecology and needs to be closely calibrated!"

Nick laughed scornfully. "What you don't realize, and what even he doesn't grasp is that it is no longer an experiment in environmental ecology. It's entirely a matter of genetic control now."

"Nick," said Izzy, "You haven't done anything to the genetic protocols, have you?"

"Done anything? You plodder, I've surpassed them. Do you really think I spent all that time since the reptile fiasco twiddling my thumbs? The reptiles had already shown AI, full self awareness through artificial intelligence. I saved everything essential I had done with the DNA and since then I have been honing it and perfecting it in a few snakes I kept on my own. Think we can't use snakes to get mammalians to think a different way? Think again!"

Gabi frowned. "But they're already self-aware. So your artificial intelligence stuff wouldn't give them anything they didn't have already."

"Oh, I've gone far beyond that. Self-awareness is one thing, but I've made their selves into something one step further, I've found a way to implant a self-motivating pleasure principle in them that will override all other drives."

The others gazed in shocked silence for a minute. Then Mike spoke. "But with creatures of that order, they'll never survive, they'll self-destruct."

"Not before I'm ready for them to do it. I want to pique them to try a few new things first. Then I'll harvest the results, as I did from the reptiles."

Izzy nodded his head. "That's why the mating protocols broke down. Your pleasure principle has overcome their most basic instincts and sent them off on a search for constant stimulation that will never end." He tapped on a few computer keys. "Until the population becomes unsustainable – not that far off in the future."

Mike's brow wrinkled. "The old man will know."

"He'll know nothing of the kind. In a little while he'll saunter back in here with his head in a fog, wondering how his perfect little plans for the primates fell apart."

Izzy pressed the earphone to the side of his head. "Not in a while. Now!! The batrachians sense him approaching because of the change in the magnetic field."

Gabi leaned forward in earnest. "Tell him, Nick. Tell him right away."

Nick grinned back. "You tell him if you dare, go ahead. But remember the price. And it's going up all the time. I'll have you on your knees in no time, you skank. Just go ahead and open you big mouth."

The Boss was shaking his bushy white hair as he stepped in the door. At first he appeared not to notice the assistants, turning away from them. But then they heard his sonorous voice say, "I'm glad you're all here. We need to make some changes."

Mike stepped forward and blurted out, "Sir, there's something you need to know. Something dangerous is going on. Nick – "

"You look worried, son. Calm down. You don't need to protect me from any truth. I'm a big boy, too, you know."

Gabi interjected, "But sir, Mike's right. The entire program could be ruined, all the projects will go down the drain if – "

"Sometimes we have to let go of some things to save others, my dear young lady, that's how the system works."

"Why don't you pipe down and see what our leader has to say?" Nick smirked.

"Thank you, Nick. Always to the point as usual. Well, I've been down to the mammalian compound and I don't like what I find. They seem to have degenerated even worse than last time and I believe serious action is in order."

Izzy perked up. "Do you mean cancellation, sir? In that case, could I suggest that the protein – "

"No, Izzy, I know what you're going to ask, but I'm not going to let you feed those subjects to your frogs, especially not alive! I have my rules about how things will be done here. Besides, I am not shutting down the whole project."

Nick gave the others an I-told-you-so look.

The Boss went on. "I know that a lot of them will have to be destroyed and I have decided to eliminate those that will not continue. Better to let them perish than to pass on something to subjects in another project. After all, what is wrong with them might prove, in some manner, to be contagious."

"But it doesn't sound bacteriological," objected Mike.

"Doesn't have to be," whispered Gabi. "Could be viral, or even prionic." She glanced up at Nick. "We can't imagine what has gotten into those subjects or how."

"In any case, I have given the lot a good look over," said the Boss. "I've culled out a number that might serve for a new control group. Not many, mind you, but more than I thought at first. We'll have to go right back to the drawing board with them and work on the most basic adaptations to the environment. With a sharpening of the selective eugenics and some behavioral conditioning, all might not be lost. I'm planning to take a hand myself from now on. Directly back into the handiwork. I've always missed that anyway."

Nick chimed in. "I'm glad you're thinking of a little shakeup, sir. I have a few suggestions of my own I'd like to discuss with you. It seems to me that we could realize some interesting economies by consolidation. I could certainly take on a lot more – "

"Yes, Nick, I believe you can."

Izzy would not give up his quest for protein, though. "Sir, in the most strenuous terms, I must object to the waste of good biological resources when there is so much to be gained from the batrachian experiment." He glanced at Nick. "I realize some people feel that I haven't brought them far enough, and I am completely ready to step aside, provided that the work go on. Just listen to their music, sir, and think what the right nutrients might – "

"I know they may not make the kind of cognitive progress you want without that metabolism, Izzy, but I want you to look at some other survival factors first."

"Sir," answered the desperate amphibiologist, "We have here a breakthrough from biology into culture of unprecedented importance. You cannot let the chance slip though your fingers."

"There are many chances, Izzy. But I won't let your subjects starve, don't worry." He scrawled out a note and handed it to the bespectacled young colleague. "Take this down to entomology and draw whatever you need from their stores."

"Oh, no, bugs and mealworms!" Izzy whined. "Their music, sir, it will just become so degraded. I can't stand by – "

The Boss drew a breath and his voice assumed a quieter but at the same time immensely more powerful tone as he slowly stated, "Izrafel, that is not a suggestion, but a direct order. Off with thee to entomology! And you, my dear Gabrielle, and you, too, Michael, can accompany him and help him bring up the stores."

"Right away, sir," acknowledged Michael, and he took Gabi by the arm as they followed a dejected Izzy toward the far doorway.

When they had filed out, Nick turned to the Boss and said, "Very clever, sir. And merciful, too, to spare them a good reaming. By way of consolidation, I would like to suggest – "

"Oh, I intend to talk about consolidation in just a bit, Nick. You'd better sit down." The Boss's tone had changed again and when Nick turned to him to scrutinize his face for the reason, he saw a look he had not seen for a long time, one that sent chills down his spine. Anger was concentrated in those eyes like a beam from a blazing fire.

The Boss reached for something in the pocket of his tweed jacket and tossed it on the table in front of Nick. Aghast, the assistant's jaw dropped, as he realized, too late, what was on the Boss's mind. The object was a skull with two enormous fangs.

"Now, Nick," said the Boss, "First we're going to have a little discussion about snakes."

Nick folded his dark wings closer to his body and hung his head, fearing, correctly, the absolute worst.

First Light

The address read: " Honr. William Wiley, Chief Constable, Westfield, Massachusetts Bay Colony. 12 June. The year of our Lord, 1735. From Gerald Bean, Magistrate's Court, Boston." So read it, again and again. Wiley had little haste to read on. News from Boston was mostly bad when it came in such official form. Holding it up to his ample nose and sniffing, Wiley was sure he could detect the faintest odor of codfish. A man who lived in the back country of America, nearly a hundred miles from the coast, had little use for such conundrums. If Wiley had wanted a life full of hustle and bustle he would have stayed in Newburyport, instead of journeying for days into the woods to have more elbow room, here on the knees of the Berkshire Hills.

"Sooner or later, you'll have to finish reading it, Will." The wry comment came from a sallow fellow sweeping the plank floor of the constable's office.

"I'll thank you to keep your opinions to yourself, Abner," hissed Wiley, as he slit the seal off with his rustic knife. He peered at the fine characters traced by a clerkish hand until he had grasped the gist of the message. "Death and damnation!" he exclaimed, "Black Ben Porter and Pirate Flowers have escaped from the Worcester jail. They're reported heading this way, making for the Hudson, and we're ordered to apprehend them. Apprehend them! And how am I supposed to apprehend anything in my condition?" He hoisted a gout-ridden leg up onto a footstool nearby.

"Don't reckon you could stop those demons if you had legs like a racehorse, Wiley," sneered Abner. "They're both cutthroats with a dozen murders between 'em. Used to sail with Captain Kidd, some people say. Not the sort you'd like to run into, Will."

"I'd strike them down, by gar," Wiley protested. "If my bum leg didn't hinder me so, I'd strike them and bind them and lead them back into Boston tied to my horse, I would."

"Ah, yah. Sure you would, Will," nodded Abner. "But for now you'd better think about how to track those critters down."

"Nothing to track a snake like another snake. Go fetch me the Injun." Wiley painfully removed his swollen limb from the footstool. "I'm going to get Nathaniel."

Leaning ponderously on his walking stick, Constable Wiley hurrumphed his way down the earthen main street of Westfield in the direction of the little cottage where his assistant lived with his widowed mother. Townspeople on their errands and farmers striding along with hoes on their shoulders called his way, "Morning, Will!" and he snorted as he passed them. He rapped his cane heartily on the cottage door, but before the fourth knock, the door suddenly opened and he was looking at the lean, horse-like countenance of Assistant Constable Nathaniel Bumppo.

"Morning, Will!" chimed the equally equine widow, peering around her beanpole of a son.

"Come in and have a cup of tea."

"Thank you, but no, Ida. Nathaniel and I have some man's business to discuss."

"Don't want to interfere with your virility none," quipped the lady, returning to her kitchen. Nathaniel ducked his head to come out the door and squinted down at Wiley. "What can I do, Sir? Need me to break up a fight?" He peered down the street looking for combatants. "It's a little early for drinkin' and rasslin' today."

"My boy, I have for you a most important and serious charge," Wiley pompously announced. "You are to lead an expedition into the woods in search for two most desperate and felonious individuals."

"Ain't done much exploring since I was mustered out of the militia after the Injun troubles," mused the youth. "Best I'd get my musket and pack ready."

"Meet me at the constabulary!"

Natty Bumppo knew as soon as he opened the constable's door that something was not right, because he smelled bear grease. He'd come to know that Indian lodge odor as a militiaman, avenging the death of his father during the frontier Wars and fighting his way up to the rank of corporal. Standing next to Wiley was a young man about his own age, barely twenty winters, shorter than he, but broad-shouldered and powerful, clad only in buckskin breeches that reached to his mocassins. On his chest a rattlesnake was vividly tattooed.

"Nathaniel, this man is going to be your tracker and guide. His name is ... Chinnacook."

"Ching-gach-gook," corrected the Indian, in distinct syllables that descended like notes of music.

Nathaniel eyed the cut of his clothes, the necklace around his throat, and the style of his smooth, black hair. "I know your kind," he said. "Mohican."

"Mohican," nodded the native. "Wolf people. You are Yen-gese, once soldier."

Bumppo was surprised that Chinggachgook had observed him even more closely, somehow guessing at his military background. "How'd you know that?"

"I watched you at the shoot before the winter moon. You won the turkey. You never missed. You have eyes like a hawk."

Nathaniel's chest puffed with pride, even at the compliment of a savage. "Nice of you to say so," he acknowledged. "Where are we bound for, sir?" he inquired, turning to Wiley.

The constable passed him the letter from Boston. "Read this carefully, for it contains a detailed description of the two men you are to arrest. Chinnachook here seems to have heard about them already, since his tribe has had a run-in with them before. Track them all up and down the Berkshires and all over the Taconic Hills if you have to, but under no circumstances are you to let them reach the Hudson River. They have friends among the Dutch there, for Pirate Flowers is Dutch himself, and they can go to ground so you'll never find them. Good hunting and good luck. Take some irons with you to bring them back in."

"Buckhide thongs are a lot lighter, thanks," replied Bumppo. He asked the Indian, "You got good store of pemmikin for the trip?" Chinggachgook nodded.

Widow Bumppo had quickly packed the two-week ration of biscuit and jerky that she kept at the ready for one of her son's forays into the great woods. Without saying more, the two young men left the dusty constabulary and strode down the westward road, one with a loping gait, the other with the agile, ball-of-the-foot step of a seasoned forest dweller. In less than ten minutes they were past the last homestead, out of earshot of the village smithy and the cowbells, beyond the smoky scent of the hearth fires, under the vast canopy of ash and maple that seemed to go on forever.

Nathaniel knew from his militia days that there were really nothing in the way of roads through the forests of western Massachusetts. There had never been a lot of contact in the interior between the Bay Colony and the formerly Dutch outposts of New Amsterdam, now New York. However, it stood to reason that the quickest way over the Berkshires and down to the settlement of Albany was through the pass called Jacob's Ladder, so it was in that direction that he and his guide naturally went, figuring to backtrack towards Worcester and catch the criminals as they approached the gap. Though his enormous legs gave him an advantage of nearly two feet per stride over the Indian, Nathaniel was soon puffing a bit to keep up, and he marveled at Chinggachgook's speed and stamina. The warrior could easily hike thirty-five or even forty miles a day if he didn't have to slow down for the assistant constable and constantly scour around for signs in the leaf mold of the forest floor.

At sundown of the second day they camped in a pass in the main range of the Berkshires. They had seen lots of game, and Bumppo had more than once been tempted to unsling his musket and shoot some fresh meat, but he could tell from the Indian's glance that they needed to maintain silence while on the trail. From what he had read about Porter and Flowers, he was very content to stay the hunter and not to become the hunted by revealing his position. Chinggachgook was more and more of a mystery to him.

The Indian strode to the top of the pass and climbed a rocky abutment, then to Bumppo's surprise stared down toward the

Hudson valley to the west, instead of to the east from where the convicts were coming.

"What's down there?" the colonist inquired.

"Shodack," Chinggachgook answered, pointing to an area across from the dimly visible settlement of Albany, which had once been the Dutch outpost of Fort Orange. "Ancient council fires of all the Wolf People. Until the Dutchmen left. Now the Iroquois hunt there. It is dead to us."

He stared down into the valley, wrapped in thoughts of a past Nathaniel could not fathom.

"Chinggachgook, what does your name mean?"

"Great serpent," the Indian said, tapping the rattler on his chest. "My spirit beast."

"Strange to call a man a beast."

"Good name. I call you Hawkeye."

"Think I'd prefer you to call me Assistant Constable Bumppo."

The Indian smiled for the first time Nathaniel could remember. "Bu-ma-po," he chuckled. "No. No. Not good thing in my tongue. Better Hawkeye."

"Bumppo is a fine Cornish name brought over by my father. No man should be ashamed of his father's name or the nature he comes by."

Chinggachgook looked at him closely. "Your father Yen-gese redcoat?"

"Neither of us was really a professional redcoat soldier, just militia. No, he was just a farmer, got killed in the last war. Greylocks' War. Up in the Green Mountains. In 1726."

Chinggachgook stared pensively into the campfire. "Mine, too. On the warpath of nations, against the French. Perhaps they died together." He raised his eyes to Bumppo's. "First the Wolf People fought beside the Yen-gese. Against Pequots. Against Iroquois. King William's War. In Canada, against the fort of Quebec. But the Yen-gese will not leave us in peace. They take more and more. The Spirit made enough for all people, but the Yen-gese kill the forest. One of our chiefs, Keepedo, has taken some of the people away far to the west. Not many Wolf People left here. Fewer and fewer fires at Wenahkutook."

Bumppo debated internally whether he should mention the Mohican attacks on Deerfield and Haverhill that his father had seen years ago. But since Chinggachgook was talking about cooperation, he decided it would be politic to try to offer a positive note. "The forest is still mighty big."

"Yes," agreed the Indian, more hopefully. "Perhaps big enough."

"Why are you on this trip? I mean, I have to do it because I'm the Assistant Constable and all. But wouldn't you rather be out hunting or something? Is it for money?"

"These men killed the sister of the woman I marry. Killed her children, too. Slow to die. We still hear them screaming." Chinggachgook's finger ran along the blade of his steel tomahawk head. "I find them. I kill them. Spirits of the family sleep quiet again."

"Now just wait a minute here, Mister Chinggachgook. You keep in mind that this here is a police expedition and you are an official constable's guide and we are authorized by the Province of Massachusetts Bay to arrest those varmints and bring them back to justice, not just slaughter them, even if they deserve it."

"You can arrest," nodded the Indian. "I will kill."

By the next afternoon, they stood looking eastward on the shoulder of the pass, with the zigzag path leading down into the Hudson Valley at their backs. In several hours of intensive scouting, they had found no trace of the fugitives having recently passed through the area. Now it remained to backtrack and try to come upon them by surprise. Nathaniel decided to follow a stream that ran down toward the Housatonic River, the best remaining approach to the passes. They moved slowly, so as not to miss their prey, but the mosquitoes in the marshes by the stream were driving Bumppo crazy. Without a fire, which would have betrayed their position, or smoke to drive away the bugs, Nathaniel scratched through a miserable night. In the morning, he opened his eyes to see Chinggachgook poking around in the leaves near his bedroll.

The Indian held up a maple leaf and shook his head. "Negh. Not good." There was fresh blood on the leaf from one of the places Bumppo had scratched raw.

Chinggachgook reached into his buckskin pouch and pulled out a small earthenware jar sealed with a lid. He handed it to the constable. When Bumppo opened it, he was at first overcome by the reek.

"Pawhh! Bear grease! No way I'm slathering that nasty stuff on me!"

Chinggachgook rubbed some on his arm and held it near a pool teeming with freshly fledged bloodsuckers. "See?" he demonstrated. "No bite. No scratch. No blood sign."

Frowning, Nathaniel dabbed some of the stuff over his insect-bitten hide and found to his surprise that something in the thick ointment also soothed the torment of the bites. "Just the same," he pouted, "I'm gonna find me a hot spring to wash this stuff off before I get back into town. I'll be the laughing stock of Westfield if I come back stinkin' like a savage."

"You come to my people, Hawkeye, to Wenahkutook, no one will laugh," smiled Chinggachgook.

Just at twilight Assistant Constable Bumppo and his guide spotted smoke from a fire, and in the deepening dusk they stealthily approached the glow next to a stream. Hidden in the underbrush, Nathaniel's sharp eyes made out a human figure shambling around the campfire.

"That thar must be Pirate Flowers, to judge from his clothes." The man was wearing a bright sash instead of a belt, with two pistols stuck into it, and a broad-brimmed hat that seemed out of place in the forest. His partner, Ben Porter, was nowhere to be seen. Bumppo turned to the Indian and said, "I'm going down there and put the bonds on that fellow before his friend comes back. That should put the odds strictly in our favor. You stay right here and don't try to come in and scalp anyone."

"Not good," snorted Chinggachgook. "You know not where that other man is. Better attack two in sight, not one seen, one hiding."

"That's the kind of Injun thinkin' that gets nothin' done on time. The chief sent me out to bring those varmints back and they're not payin' by the hour. You just stay here out of sight and don't get in my way." Chinggachgook did not return his stare, gazing off into the greenery on the other side of the hill.

Nathaniel made his way down towards the stream, carefully avoiding dry sticks, clinging vines, or other obstacles that might give away his movements. He felt proud of himself for approaching the fire without detection and readied his rifle to make the arrest. When Flowers, busying himself with some cooking chores, had turned his back, he stepped into the clearing and announced, "You're under arrest, Flowers. Stop in the name of the law. Don't reach for those guns or I'll blow a hole through your head."

The former corsair turned and faced the policeman with a smile. "Well, now, no reason to be rude, son, none at all," he chortled. "Flowers knows when he's been had, he does. I don't need no airing out, I'll tell you dat. Why not I make you some of dese eggs before we start off, huh, no use letting dem go to waste, dey's mighty good!"

"Don't need no supper. Where's that friend of yours, Porter?"

"Porter?" bellowed the pirate, "Why dat boy's gone out and got drunk on rum. He's out dere somewheres in de woods, drunk like a pig. You'll sniff him out on the way back for sure."

"Keep your voice down if you want to live," cautioned Bumppo. "Now you just get down on the ground and spread out your arms and legs real slow."

"Aw, please, captain," retorted Flowers, "I got mighty bad knees from my days at sea and I can't get down on dat ground so fast. Why not you come over and just tie up my hands. I don't do nuttin' bad."

"I said get on the ground!"

"No, please, boss, don't make me hurt my old knees. I can help you when we get old Porter. Maybe he'll show up. Hey, dat might be him now, by golly! Look dere!"

Bumppo's eyes darted in the direction Flowers pointed and saw a red hat poking up above the bushes. He pivoted his long musket and aimed to shoot right between the eyes. No sooner had his weapon discharged than he heard an almost simultaneous shot and felt a terrible pain in his left leg, causing him to crumple to the ground. In a split second Flowers was next to him with his frying pan in hand. Bumppo had barely turned his head toward him when he felt a tremendous jolt to the side of his skull. For the only time in his young life, he experienced defeat and, almost immediately, unconsciousness.

    The first thing Nathaniel Bumppo did when he came to was to reach to touch the searing feeling in his leg. He did not get far. Rapidly he discovered that he was firmly bound to a tree at the edge of the clearing. The second thing he did was shiver, which led him to the realization that he was almost naked. A considerable time must have gone by since his attempt to take Flowers into custody, for it was now deep night. It took a few seconds for him to grasp the desperation of his position. His eyes were still swimming from the blow Flowers had struck him with the frying pan, but he gradually made out that there were now two figures passing a jug next to the fire. Flowers, with his colorful rags and flowing beard, came into focus, then Porter, with a long, broken nose, grimy face, and unkempt hair. Debris from a meal scattered around the campsite showed that it was now long past dinnertime. A jab of pain from the leg made him moan and that brought his captors sauntering over toward him.

Flowers was the most garrulous of the two, that was clear. "By gar," he said, "Dis brave police feller is coming back to life. I t'ought we'd lost you dere, matey! Oh, I forgot to tell you, Ben, we's under arrest!"

The two felons howled with laughter. Then Flowers went on. "You be a pretty hard character, all right, lawman. I t'ink you would have put a hole right t'rough my head, like you said, but instead, you almost killed our poor, innocent girl, Nellie, and ruined her best Sunday hat." As the criminals doubled up in mirth again, Bumppo looked across the clearing and saw a donkey standing with a grazing wound on its skull and the remains of a bonnet on the ground. Flowers's loud shouts must have alerted Porter, close by and out of sight, who had the presence of mind to use the pack animal as a decoy, correctly assuming that the Assistant Constable's trigger finger would be faster than his sense.

Bumppo realized that Chinggachgook had been exactly right in his hesitation to approach the clearing without knowing the whereabouts of both suspects. "Damn redskin knows my trade better than I do," he muttered to himself, but quickly checked himself when

Porter scowled, "What you sayin'?" It would be a great mistake to reveal the one thing that could save his life now, the fact that the Indian guide might still be somewhere in the vicinity. If Porter hadn't killed him already. Or if he hadn't abandoned the overconfident white man.

"Water," croaked the captive, "Give me something to drink for pity's sake."

"Now, matey," smirked Flowers, "You weren't going to take no pity on me for my poor knees. Now your own ain't in such good shape at all, no." He poked the wound with a stick, causing Bumppo to howl. "I reckon you got you a broken leg along with a pistol ball in there. Gonna be real hard for you to move. Not so, Porter?"

"That's so," nodded the slovenly comrade. "Guess we won't be able to get you to no proper doctor."

"No," agreed Flowers, reaching for his pistol, "I t'ink it's time for what de Frenchies call de coup de grace. I'll make it quick for you, sonny."

"Belay that, Flowers!" scowled Porter, who drew a wicked looking cutlass from a scabbard at his belt. "I might want to try to operate myself. I bet I'd be a real good doctor. Course I'm gonna have to remove considerable skin first to see what I'm doin'. I'll start right up here at the groin for practice."

Porter's face was now a sadistically distorted rictus of pleasure and Nathaniel realized too late that the quiet degenerate was the more dangerous of the escapees. Just as the blade approached his skin, he heard Flowers say, "Wait, Porter, lookee over dere!" The two captors were staring at the stream. When Bumppo succeeded in moving his head a little to the side, he could see a light coming down the little valley, slowly, turning sometimes from side to side, but always descending towards the camp.

"Damned if dis puppy didn't have some help close by!" exclaimed Flowers.

Porter sheathed his cutlass. "Keep him alive for a while. We might want him to call those others over here. Let's hide in there and watch them." The convicts slipped into the shrubs on the opposite end of the clearing, by the stream.

A few seconds later, Bumppo felt his bonds suddenly become a little looser. Before he could start to struggle, he heard a voice behind him say, "No moves! No talk!" He smelled bear grease. Chinggachgook was behind the tree, cutting him loose. He wondered how the Indian planned to move his injured body to safety from the murderers. Meanwhile, the light had gotten much closer and Flowers and Porter were cocking their pistols. Still, there were no signs of men. Bumppo wondered what allies his guide had pressed into service to effect his rescue. Suddenly the source of the light came into view. A little wooden ark bearing a fire of twigs emerged from behind a rock, floating in the stream. Chinggachgook had built this little fire ship to draw away the enemy's attention.

"What de hell is dat ting?" yelled Flowers, as the murderers emerged to get a better view. While their eyes were turned to the stream, Bumppo felt a powerful grasp raise him into the air and bear him into the dark underbrush.

Behind him, he heard Porter shout, "He's getting away!"

Flowers swore, "He won't get far wit dat leg!" The two came crashing into the bushes in pursuit.

Suddenly Bumppo felt he was on the ground, then dragged under the ground, beneath a giant boulder. Soundlessly, Chinggachgook slid a smaller rock into the opening, sealing them in. The Mohican said nothing, so neither did Nathaniel, though his leg smarted with hellish suffering. He was not about to let it be said that he couldn't stay just as quiet as any Injun when the situation called for it. Outside, the criminals thrashed about, cursing, leaving the area in peace for a few minutes, then coming back. Bumppo eventually gave in to weakness and pain and fell asleep.

What seemed like a long time later, he felt something shaking him awake. There was light. The small stone was rolled back and Chinggachgook was easing him out the opening of what he now recognized to be a bear's winter den. The Indian had used his forest lore to find it and arranged it as a nearby hideout where he could hide the wounded man instead of trying a futile race to freedom. Finally, the crooks had given up and headed on toward New York in the daylight. Bumppo realized that his leg hurt less and was astonished to see that, in the dark, Chinggachgook had eased the ball out of the flesh with his knife and applied a poultice of herbs and some kind of muck to the wound.

He almost gave a whoop of pleasure. But he stopped himself and said, instead, "Chinggachgook, you are some deep woods doctor! I thought I was a goner there for a while. Now we can catch up with those varmints and put 'em in bonds."

But before he could try to get on his feet, Chinggachgook checked him with a firm hand on his arm. "No travel now. Time to eat."

"What do you mean, eat, man, we've got work to do?"

Chinggachgook looked at him as he might look at a wayward child. Slowly he explained, "If you eat not, you die; you eat now, tonight you travel. Tomorrow you use this." He thrusted his arm in the air, holding Bumppo's musket, which he must have managed to snatch earlier when the fugitives were not looking.

Nathaniel had to admit that the Mohican seemed to be right again. Besides, he mused, how was he, wounded, going to take two desperate, well-armed, healthy criminals into custody? Maybe the Indian was still dead-bent on sneaking up on the outlaws by night and cutting their throats. Then again, he thought to himself, maybe it would serve those boys right. After all, they had been on the point of skinning him alive. Maybe the niceties of law and order were less important than simply stopping those two monsters before they had a chance to do more harm. All at once, Westfield seemed very far behind. If there was going to be a new law out here in the forest, it was clear that Chinggachgook had to be a part of it. Right now the Mohican was much more fit than Bumppo to perform some sort of action, and the white man resolved that, whatever it was, his place was to go along and help as best he could. He smiled and gratefully accepted the jerky and pemmikin that Chinggachgook offered him, taking some consolation that the absence of fire meant that their stealthy pursuit was not over.

After the meal, they slept most of the day under the shade of the trees. When the sun was well down they started up the valley in the direction Flowers and Porter had gone. Before long they had found signs of a rest stop by the fleeing pair, feces of donkey and men and a broken bottle, proof that the convicts had had a little celebration while they surveyed the lower slopes for signs of possible pursuers. There was blood, too. Perhaps Nellie's head wound was not healing well, causing Flowers and Porter to slow down. The criminals were taking their time now, enjoying the food and loot they had probably taken from some settlers who would be found murdered, sooner or later.

In the dark the tracking continued, with very little time lost as Chinggachgook uncannily managed to find marks where Bumppo could barely make out boulders and trees to avoid, as he hobbled along with the crutch the Mohican had fashioned from a sapling. Deep into the night, descending another ridge, they perceived the distant glow of a campfire and hope sprang up in Bumppo's heart that perhaps the capture could be made after all. Just before daybreak, as the stars were beginning to fade, Chinggachgook stopped and turned to his partner.

"My time to go now. No prisoners. I kill one, maybe two. You stay here with your hawkeye musket. Watch if I chase one this way." He paused and cast a glance at the white man. "You will kill? Not just arrest?"

"No, you're right, my friend, I'll not try to be a hero any more. If that skunk comes out of the bushes, I'll kill him right away and do as I'm told."

The Mohican nodded and slipped away. It seemed like hours as the silence persisted. On the positive side, Bumppo thought this might be good, since the Indian was much more likely to make a silent kill than were his prey. Then a shot rang out. A few seconds later another. Then, after a minute, a third. There was no movement near the dying fire, and nothing emerged from the bushes. After another seemingly interminable interval, Bumppo heard

Chinggachgook's voice from the shadows, "I come!"

"I'll hold my fire," he answered.

The Mohican emerged from the leaves, blood covering much of his chest, and more leaking from a nasty slash on his leg. "One escaped."

The Indian had succeeded in jumping one of the pair just as they were moving out of camp. Pistols had not been able to save Flowers. But during the fight, Porter had been able to land a blow with his cutlass, hobbling the attacker almost as badly as Bumppo had been.

"There'll be little chance of capturing Black Ben now, with both of us bummed up like this," sighed Nathaniel, but Chinggachgook exclaimed, "Look!"

On a cliffside leading out of the valley, which must have been the last rocky barrier between the Berkshires and the downslope of the Taconics, Porter was climbing to freedom. Another twenty yards and he could go over the crest and follow the Fishkill or some other stream down to the Dutch country. He would be out of range and out of jurisdiction.

Bumppo turned to Chinggachgook and said, "You did well. You fought well. I'm proud to be with you." He paused and looked up the hill. "Can you catch that other one?"

Chinggachgook shook his head. "Too far for me." But he pointed up the slope and added, "You shoot him!"

"But that's a good furlong!" The Mohican didn't answer.

"That's maybe 300 yards. An awful hard shot."

"You shoot him."

Quickly Bumppo unloaded his gun and re-cleaned it, inserting new powder and searching his pouch for the best, most perfect ball he could find. He reloaded and trained his sights on the cliff. Porter was almost at the top. Resisting the urge to fire, he calculated the wind and offset for the extra range the ball would have to travel. Meanwhile, Porter's arms were grasping the lip of the rock and then they were heaving his body over. At the crest, the outlaw suddenly paused, drew himself up, and looked back in triumph over his helpless pursuers. He couldn't resist the chance to gloat. It was then, with the target silhouetted against the brightening sky, that Bumppo pulled the trigger. The explosion, the smoke, the sound echoed on the hills, but on the crest nothing seemed to happen. All at once, the dark body of the murderer appeared to crumble and it slowly swayed over the brink of the cliff before plunging onto the boulder-strewn slope below.

Bumppo drew a long breath. Chinggachgook gave a little nod of satisfaction. "You fight well, too. I am proud to be by your side."

Nathaniel was filled with such a good feeling that he almost reached out and hugged the Mohican, but he stopped just in time and just nodded, "Yup, yup, I did. We both did. We're quite a pair aren't we? I wonder if a… if our people ever did so well before, together?"

Then, smiling with a little embarrassment, he added, "I guess we ought to get our sorry selves back somewhere before the buzzards have us for lunch. It's sure not goin' to be easy stumpin' our way back down through the woods."

The Mohican gave a triumphant cry and plunged back into the bushes, emerging a minute later with Nellie, who did not look so worse for the wear now. "This ugly horse carries us now," stated the Indian.

"Let's go see your medicine men before we bleed to death."

Two weeks later Nathaniel Bumppo and Chinggachgook emerged from the deep woods into the cleared land outside of Westfield. Their wounds were tolerably healed after a stay in the Mohican home village of Wenahkutook. The return to Westfield was far different from Nathaniel's cocky departure. Now the white man was dressed entirely in native buckskin: new leggings, fringed jacket and well-wrought mocassins. His ragged woolens had been torn up or burned. The two men now moved out of the underbrush as a team, stepping in tandem and each scanning his side of the trail. There were changes within, as well. Nathaniel had been worrying for days about how to tell his mother about Sparrow Woman, who had cared for him, applying remedies only those first forest people knew. After the inevitable dances and Chinggachgook's campfire recital of their fight with Porter and Flowers, she had come to him in the lodge at night and given him her body, letting him know that he was a worthy man and a champion. Their short, tender time together had dispelled from his mind all the frontier gossip he had heard about squaws. How would he discuss this passion with a righteous Christian mother, after doing things and feeling things he would never have imagined a civilized Christian boy would feel and do?

He was shaken from his reverie by a boisterous "Halloo!" from the direction of the town. A small delegation clustered around his limping superior, Will Wiley, was hurrying out to meet them.

"Good work, young Natty! That redskin messenger from the Stockbridge mission you sent ahead reached us yesterday. A mission accomplished and a great deed of justice done!" boomed the chief constable.

"I'm mighty pleased you're happy with it, sir."

"Happy? Of course, I'm overjoyed. Westfield's constabulary will be the talk of the whole colony. There are rumors of advancement for myself, due to my not inconsiderable role in the apprehension of those blackguards."

"Reckon it's sure deserved, sir."

"Oh, don't think that you won't have your own share of the honor, my young protegee. As I rise in administration, I shall tow you along with me. If the expected promotions come through, I intend to nominate you to fill my shoes here in this fine town."

"Hope it won't be with all the difficulty your own feet have in there," mused Bumppo to himself. But out loud he cautioned, "Well, I think we need to have a little talk about that. Not that I'm ungrateful, but I dreadfully need to talk with my mother first about some future things. So if you'll excuse me now, I'll just..."

Nathaniel was about to stride toward his cottage when he felt a hand on his shoulder. Suddenly the constable adopted a much softer and more genuine tone. "Son, listen, it's been nigh a month and we have had a very evil time in your absence."

"What's wrong?"

"We all tried to do as well as we could. It struck soon after you left, a hideous coughing fever. At one point we were all of us sorely ailing."

"What has that to do with me?" Nathaniel glanced at his friend Chinggachgook, who had been following the conversation. Saying nothing, he made a discreet sign with his left hand, the snuffing of a flame. He had already guessed Wiley's meaning.

"Natty, you mother gave comfort like an angel of mercy. But finally she, too, was struck down. To speak plainly, her soul now resides in heaven with Christ and the saints, I am sure, and her mortal husk lies in the churchyard. I am truly sorry."

Stunned by this shocking news, Nathaniel hung his head and was motionless for some time. When he looked up again, only the Mohican still stood by his side. He signaled

Chinggachgook to follow him to the cemetery, where he knelt at a fresh grave and spent the rest of the afternoon praying. Approving of this silent grief, Chinggachgook sat many yards away and waited.

When nightfall arrived, the pair went to the widow Bumppo's cottage. However, the whispering town was amazed to see no smoke rise from the chimney, but instead a fire in the yard, where both men slept under the stars rather than seeking a good, comfortable bed under a solid British roof.

Gossip increased before dawn the next day. In a dim fog, the earliest farmers to rise and set out to milk the cows saw the bereaved, still dressed in his forest attire, knock at the Constable's office. As lamps were hastily lit and neighbors visited, those who were watching saw the parson and the notary, hastily summoned before breakfast, arrive at that solemn conclave. The townspeople would soon learn that Nathaniel had asked for a contract to be drawn up wherein Wiley would act as agent for the sale of the Bumppo homestead and trustee of the proceeds, to be held in trust until the heir saw fit to claim them. In the gloom, citizens crowded outside the office discussing these surprising developments, but none followed the young man and his companion as they slipped away toward the edge of the settlement. They were fearful of something unexpected that they didn't understand, but they already sensed that Nathaniel had brought an indelible wilderness stain back from the Berkshires and that he was going back where he now belonged, beyond them.

Chinggachgook scowled at the Westfielders as they gawked from a distance. "These people are not human beings. They offer you gold for killing men, but they do not feast you or dance your battles, they do not sing for you as we do. They show no respect and treat you like a stink-animal. Shake them off!"

To Nathaniel's surprise, Chinggachgook scraped his mocassins with a stick, removing the dust of the town.

"Well," Bumppo chuckled, "It seems to me, if I remember my Bible classes, that that was pretty fair advice from our Savior. Still, I don't hate them folk. It's in their nature, brother, the nature of the town dwellers. Used to be my nature, too. Still is, in a way."

"Because of the Mohican, I know. They want you to put off our people's clothes and our people's smell. They want to wash you with their spirit water and change you. But now you, too, are Mohican."

"You're right. It ain't just the bear grease, neither. No washin' and no baptizin' is going to change what's come over me. Mama's death was a kind of sign, because I know I could never belong here any longer. If I ever come back to Westfield, it will be to provision with powder and shot from the purse Will is keeping for me."

"So now we go hunting?"

"So now we go, my brother," answered Nathaniel in his still unfamiliar and broken Mohican dialect. They walked briskly off along the green trail that was just beginning to brighten, as the sun broke through the fog banks and illuminated the tops of the western hills.

War Games

When I turned ten years old in 1960, the world was worried about new Soviet satellites hurtling around the Earth and unseen nuclear missiles that made alert sirens sound every so often, making us dive under our desks at Bingham Elementary School for protection against atomic fallout. But after school, in the precious hours of freedom, no one on Albion Street in Somerville, Massachusetts, was worried about Reds or Communists. Instead, we refought the War to End All Wars against the real enemy of mankind, the Yellow Peril. There was no discussion about why the Japanese had to be the enemy, rather than the Germans or the Italians – it had always been that way, probably ever since previous generations of Somervillians had heard about Pearl Harbor.

And while the city had a few German-Americans like myself and forty thousand Italian-Americans, there seemed to be no Japanese-Americans anywhere in its borders to take offense. Like professional wrestling, our war games made villains of those who weren't present. On Albion Street we were fortunate to have a cruel, exemplary, and cunning enemy in the person of Charlie McSweeney.

Charlie was a genuine Juvenile Delinquent, suspended from school countless times and held back two grades. Rumor had it that he acted as a lookout for Butchie Molloy's gang when they stole hubcaps or shoplifted from the stores in Davis Square. For this reason, Charlie was already persona non grata at Papadopoulos's grocery on the end of the street. Apart from these natural qualifications, Charlie had everything he thought he needed to portray the ideal "Jap," a vision of history he got from watching *We're Coming Back to Bataan*, *Sands of Iwo Jima*, and *Halls of Montezuma* over and over again. First came an ant-like swarm of followers to be his troops. The oldest of five McSweeney boys, he could also count on the four Cousin McSweeneys who lived in the walk-up tenement one floor above him, and the Cotter brothers and the Morrisons and four or five friends from Alpine Terrace. Moreover,

Charlie McSweeney worked hard at being a "Jap" and he loved it. He would tape up the corners of his eyes with Scotch tape and smile in a buck-toothed way, using wax Halloween teeth. He insulted everyone and strutted around with a swagger stick like Sesue Hayakawa in *The Bridge on the River Kwai*, even though the stick was just part of a broken umbrella. He actually had a sort of uniform, consisting of a stiff kepi cap and a faded khaki jacket he had found in an Army-Navy store. In true "Nip" fashion, he attacked only by surprise, so we Americans had to be on guard any day after school, ready for their onslaught.

Our Marine unit consisted of myself and my best friend, Tommie De Loria, Ernie Gubbio and his little brother, the Pulsifers, Phil Billedoux, and our leader, Mikie Milano. As soon as we got changed after school, we usually ran directly to our base in De Loria's back yard. Although dangerously close to Alpine Terrace and the lair of the McSweeneys, it was a mighty and impregnable fortress, surrounded by ten foot, wire-topped fences on three sides and by Grandma De Loria's porch on the other. Any "Nip" with half a brain would rather face that barbed wire than risk getting within range of Grandma and her broom. Back in our base, we would go through a brief boot camp, which consisted of Mikie making us do jumping jacks. Then we would collect ammo.

The rules of war were simple and there were two kinds of ammo: little pebbles the size of your thumb nail for bullets, and grenades, which were actually mud balls. Our Marine-issue mud balls were made only from regulation sticky clay found in Pulsifers' back yard. The Jap grenades were, predictably, much less trustworthy. Rickie Cotter was the chief "Japanese" munition-maker and claimed to be an expert on mud balls "because he was Irish." He would always shout out as he heaved a grenade, "Hey Joe, here comes one with a surprise in it!" This usually meant a roofing nail or a wad of gross, Cotter-chewed gum. However, Chuckie was also rumored to put pieces of dog turd in his mud balls, a form of germ warfare deplored by all the Marines as being typical of "Nip dirty fighting." The De Lorias, Milanos, and Gubbios took this so much to heart that they invented a new term for dog turds and called them "Irish surprises" whenever they saw them on the street. Some of us called them "Cotters" when Rickie wasn't around.

Having made up a good supply of ammo, we stockpiled it back in the base, which was watched over by little Al Pulsifer, who was asthmatic and really wasn't supposed to play, and Tommie's sister Teresa. Teresa doubled with Al as a medic and also as guard for any prisoners we took. She was the subject of much criticism from the "Japs," who mocked us for using a girl guard. However she was a specialist in hand-to-hand combat and her vicious nails were more than a match for any unarmed captives left in her care. Actually, she almost never had to resort to violence because our prisoners were well cared for. Grandma De Loria would always come out to cast a suspicious Sicilian eye over any that were assembled in the back yard, and if Teresa assured her they were being good, Grandma would give her a tray of chocolate cookies to pass around. Very unlike the treatment *we* got. If we were caught, we were stuffed into a huge, ill-smelling refrigerator crate called the Hoosgow that sat in McSweeneys' back yard. In summer, Charlie would pour in jars full of red ants to torture the victims. Sometimes he and his brothers would jump on the box to squash any prisoners inside. To avoid getting flattened by Charlie's giant rear end, I worked out an effective way of getting all the prisoners in the Hoosgow to sway together and tip the box back, causing our tormentor to land on the ground. At the same time, we moaned and shrieked to make him believe he had really done some damage. Otherwise, he would keep on jumping just out of spite.

  Mikie always chose either Phil or me as the Scout. I loved this job, which involved concealment and sneaking around, but in truth it was not very hard, because McSweeney and his "Japs" showed a total lack of imagination and could always be found assembling in his back yard or the playground next to it. Mikie, who was actually a terrible officer, would always give the same orders if they hadn't moved yet: form a line and attack! This was of course in the brave Marine tradition, but it never, ever worked because we were outnumbered two to one and the enemy had some fine pitching arms bombarding us with mud balls. Charlie McSweeney himself was a formidable foe, firing out "bullets" at a furious pace and insisting on leading their human wave charges in person. You held your plastic or wooden rifle in your glove hand and used your throwing arm to sling pebbles, which were bullets. Pebble bullets could wound but never kill. To count a "kill," the combattant had to advance within reach, like a Sioux warrior taking coup, and fire three imaginary shots, pronouncing "Pow! Pow! Pow!" The "killed" soldier had to admit to being killed and immobilize himself, but he was allowed the histrionics of a death scene, which in some cases, like that of Phil Billedoux, assumed the proportions of Laurence Olivier. Phil could writhe and clutch for five minutes; by comparison, Richard III merely died in his sleep.

    Under the hail of mud balls we crouched behind hedges or trash cans, enduring the long range artillery and the Taunting that inevitably came with it. Just like in the movies, the "Japs" would call out to try to get us to show ourselves: "Hey, Joe, tonight you die! Death toooo Marrr-iiines! Die Yankee pigs!" Once Ernie Gubbio got so flustered by these calls and by the surprise-laden mud balls exploding on his plastic helmet that he actually went a little crazy with fear, like Robert Wagner in *Halls of Montezuma*. He ran over and surrendered himself to Charlie's gang, who immediately led him to the Hoosgow.

    Sometimes as we "dug in," we would speculate on strange, philosophical subjects. "I wonder if it would be better to be fighting real 'Japs'?"

    "Real ones would not be as bad as Charlie."

    "They're plenty bad in the movies."

    "Those guys in the movies are not even real Japs. My uncle told me they're all

Albanians or something with makeup on. All the real Japs were in jail."

"No they weren't, they were in Japan, stupid."

"If the real Japs were here, we couldn't call them Japs unless we really wanted to insult them."

"How do you know? Maybe that's what they call themselves. Or maybe Nips? Isn't Japan the Japanese name for Nippon?"

"If real Japs were here, they wouldn't be mad at us, they'd be made at Charlie McSweeney."

"I have a feeling they'd probably be mad at us, too."

One day at the end of summer there was considerable commotion on the playground and Al Pulsifer came to tell me that Charlie McSweeney had something real important to tell me about the start of school. Ordinarily I did not even talk with the McSweeneys outside of military conflict situations, but school was considered such a menace to the common good that it outweighed ordinary practices and prejudices. I went to hear what Charlie had to say. He leered at me, savoring the bad news he was waiting to unleash.

"Hey, Gainesey, you got a new teacher in your grade and are you gonna hate it, 'cause he's a Jap!"

"You're crazy. That ain't so."

"Is so, so! I seen him myself."

"How could you see anything like that? School doesn't start till Monday."

"My mother had to take me in early on account of getting my suspension lifted from last spring and I saw him right there and he was definitely a Jap, just like in the movies. Old Adolph probably brought him in specially to help him." In my mind, I had to concede that this was a logical conclusion, given the commonly held idea that our principal, Mr. Buckley, was really Adolf Hitler, who had escaped after the War and was hiding out in Somerville, though he didn't take the trouble to shave off his characteristic little moustache, almost the only one in the city. The possibility of a new Axis alliance was not out of the question.

"You're lyin'," I retorted, unwilling to give McSweeney any public credit. "Anyway, my teacher is somebody named Walker."

"That's probably some spy name he gave, but I saw him. You're gonna get flunked by a sneaky Jap!"

"I don't believe you and I ain't gonna flunk. I don't care if the teacher is Fu Manchu."

As I walked away, I heard him taunt me from behind, "Ha! Gainesey, tonight you die, Joe, you get F."

The trouble was that Charlie was at least partly right. When I showed up in fifth grade on the first day of school, there was definitely an Asian-looking man at the head of the class. It turned out when he wrote his name on the blackboard that it was not Walker, but Waka, though the pronunciation in suburban Boston was identical. Like most of the class, I was pretty stupefied and kept quiet the whole first week. Outside during recess, the catcalls started, as the McSweeneys, who had yet to get their first suspension of the year, jeered, "Hey Mr. Waka, you want some flied lice?" or "Tojo, you surrender now?" But Mr. Waka had a true poker face and it was impossible to tell if he even heard these insults. Everybody was just waiting for him to do something to prove how sneaky and deceitful he really was, betraying his true nature by participating in one of Mr. Buckley's beloved caning sessions or ratting out somebody for fighting on school grounds.

Ironically, it was I, a Marine, who first got to see what he was really made of.

On the second Wednesday after Labor Day I was engaged, along with about four other young thugs, in the innocent prankish activity of holding the basement exit door closed so the kids coming from the lunch room couldn't get outside for recess. All at once, my co-conspirators (who I later realized were all McSweeney affiliates) bolted from the door, leaving me all alone against an irresistible force that turned out to be none other than Old Adolf himself, cane in hand, looking for the culprit. I took off like a scalded dog, hoping he hadn't seen my face, raced around the side of the building and in the first floor door, looking for someplace to hide, but he was hard on my heels, tromping up the wooden steps only seconds behind me.

With all other avenues blocked, I sped for the music room, but pulled up short. There was Mr. Waka right in front of me. I could see it all: the gleeful and treacherous denunciation ("Here he is Mr. Buckley. I got him for you! Shall I hold him while you apply the cane?"), the two of them leading me off to have the backs of my hands caned before the class and then the embarrassment of my parents coming for me ("Is your son raised to be a hoodlum, Mrs. Gaines?). In Charlie's words, I was gonna die.

But instead of blocking me or grabbing me, Mr. Waka deftly swept me past him into the music room door and closed it before I realized what had happened. Outside, he was quickly confronted by Mr. Buckley.

"Oh, hello, Arthur," Mr. Waka's voice said in a deadpan tone, "Were you going in to use the piano? I didn't know you played."

"Of course not," Buckley's rat-like voice shot back. "I was after one of those little creeps who were holding the door shut. Did you see a boy come running up here?"

"Nobody ran past me," said Mr. Waka, which was technically true, since I hadn't quite run past him. "I was probably too wrapped up in my *étude* to hear all the commotion."

"Hmphh," snorted Buckley. "Well, next time try to keep an eye open and help with discipline around here. Stop fooling around with piano tunes and help us get these young animals under control. Sometimes I think I'm the only one trying to maintain a little order and dignity in this damned place."

I waited behind the door, listening to Buckley's receding footsteps and an instant later heard a couple of light knocks on the door signaling, I supposed, all clear. When I peered out, no one was there.

Now that I had become personally involved and was actually beholding to someone who may be a "Jap," I had to get to the bottom of things. I waited until the class was empty at the end of school and approached Mr. Waka's desk. He paid no attention and went on grading some papers. I cleared my throat and began: "Mr. Waka, is it true you're a.....Where are you from?"

"I'm from Oregon, out on the West Coast," he answered, matter-of-factly, turning over another paper.

"Well, I didn't think you were from around here by the way you talk." I thought I'd better find out more. "Were you ever...in the army?"

"No, actually, my dad was a Unitarian minister and so I am what you call a conscientious objector, which means I didn't fight, but I was in the medical corps for a few months in Korea."

"Oh." I imagined him alongside Teresa De Loria tending the wounded, but the idea seemed too ridiculous. I was running out of things to say. "Well...do you know karate or anything like that?"

Finally he made a wry little smile and said, "I'm really not any good at it. How about you? Do you play the piano?"

"Oh, no, Mrs. Phelps in third grade said I couldn't play anything. Last year at the hearing test they marked me deaf, but that was only because they didn't explain I was supposed to raise my hand if I heard that bell sound."

"I'm glad you're not deaf. At least you can enjoy listening to music."

"Thanks," I muttered. I wasn't sure if he knew what I was thanking him for, because he acted like nothing had ever happened. I was feeling too awkward to try to say anything else. But from that moment on I decided I was going to enjoy his class.

The next morning at recess I confronted the McSweeneys on the playground.

"You can't make those catcalls about Mr. Waka anymore."

"And why not? Ain't he a Jap?"

"Nope. He's from someplace out west and he was on our side in the army."

"He wasn't in no army! He fight for Rising Sun on Iwo Jima."

"That shows how much you know, you stupid oaf! He was in the army fighting Commies."

This caused a lot of murmuring among the McSweeney's, who had recently heard about Khrushchev and Stalin from some radio program, since they certainly couldn't read a newspaper or a real book. Mr. Waka's status as a "Jap" could not go on if he wasn't really a legitimate villain.

Charlie turned to me and tried one last ploy to rescue his pastime of Jap-baiting. "I bet you're full of baloney. How come we don't know he's just a jerk?"

So I told them the story about what happened at the music room door. Actually I exaggerated it a little bit, too. I said Mr. Waka stood in Buckley's way and shielded me from his swinging cane. McSweeney jaws were dropping as I described the scene.

Charlie resisted, "Oh yah? How do I know that's true?"

"He called him Arthur." This left my interlocutors dumbfounded. I don't know what perplexed them more: the idea that someone could treat Mr. Buckley, Der Fuhrer himself, on a first-name basis, or the possibility that he wasn't Adolf, after all. I saw my advantage and decided to go for the final point. "I think he threatened to give Buckley a karate chop." There was nothing more to say. I walked off and could practically hear the rusty gears grinding in the McSweeney heads behind me.

For most of that fall there were no more after school or weekend games of War. The McSweeneys were left without an identity, dolts without a country who could no longer play the role of Japs with any hope of verisimilitude. They also stopped the catcalls and watched Mr. Waka closely, interpreting any remotely graceful gesture as a secret karate move. Instead, they infuriated Mr. Buckley so much with dialectal playground calls of "Hey, Ahh-thuhhh!" that he shaved off the moustache to try to change his image. He was too embarrassed to cane anyone any more.

Charlie McSweeney was at a loss what to do. He couldn't bring himself to restyle the gang as Krauts, because he couldn't stomach taking on the personality of Hitler, even though Mr. Buckley had apparently vacated that role. A brief hint that the villains might be restyled as Wops led to a massive and definite veto from Mikie Milano, the Gubbios and especially the De Lorias, who threatened to tell Grandma. This scared Charlie more than anything.

The problem was finally solved by Mother Nature, when a November storm swept down out of Canada and dumped a couple of feet of early snow on Greater Boston. We emerged the next day after the plows had done their work and found they had heaped up a giant mountain of snow right next to the McSweeney residence in Alpine Terrace. The ant-like horde of followers was busy at work making an arsenal of snow grenades. Of course, we knew that a lot of them would have cores of dirty ice or other Cotter inventions. On top of the pile stood Charlie McSweeney, defying the world. Gone were the faded khakis, the kepi hat, and the taped-up eyelids, replaced by a big, ratty fur coat, a moth-eaten pair of earmuffs, and a size 12 shoe that he pounded and pounded on the snow packed in front of him, ranting just like Nikita K at the UN.

"Americanski svine, ve vill bury you. Ve vill send you to Siberia. You vill freeze in our Red Hoosgow. Ve vill stuff ice down your Yankee troats. Hey, Joe, tonight you vill die!!"

Under the Lens

L ouis de Montalte-Königsbourg arrived in Ozone State University looking for trouble, as powerful and unsuspected an intruder as one of the tornadoes that swept in from the Gulf of Mexico at night, looking for trailer parks to ravage. At first, as with the storms, there was just a tiny puff of cloud on the horizon. We all remember that two years ago, a rumor buzzed slowly as a November bumblebee through the clammy yellow brick classroom blocks of the campus that some foreign professor from another country had requested through a federal grant program that he be assigned to Ozone. That had never happened at Ozone before. President Martin Otto, popularly known on campus as Palindrome, fired off a memo to department heads ordering that some volunteer be found for an exchange with the "Sourbone School, in Paris, France," or else.

Bill Hawkins, an English professor very low in the pecking order and Second Assistant Baseball Coach for the Ozone Snarling Peccaries (who had finished the last season 5 and 38) was promptly volunteered and shipped off to a language lab in Paris, much to the mystification and amusement of his new French colleagues.

Sure enough, there at the annual faculty convocation in August was President Palindrome, flushed with the pride of new international recognition, for now he could brag of having attracted a faculty member from out of state. It was with distinct pleasure that he introduced "Professer Lewie di Mount-alltie Cone-is-berg." Everyone on the staff saw and heard this celebrity presentation, since the annual convocation was one of three events in the academic year that had to be attended upon pain of immediate dismissal from the university. President Palindrome's cousin, Representative Huff McFard, had actually shoved a law to this effect through the state legislature during one of its more torpid moments.

However, at the grand convocation, the bespectacled, balding, wimpish figure that

Palindrome was slapping on the back did not look very important. In fact, he looked a little like the guy in the old Charles Atlas Body Building commercials that always got sand kicked in his face by bullies at the beach. There was an audible sigh of disappointment from the soccer and tennis factions in the faculty who had somehow developed the idea that the new man was a sort of incipient Pele or Bjorn Borg, who had chosen Ozone specifically to train for a world championship in one of the less-manly-sports. It was clear that this unprepossessing character would never be seen on the athletic field or in the gym for the time-honored campus ritual of Thursday afternoon intramurals. All of his fellow teachers, who had as much trouble with his moniker as the President, immediately baptized him Lewie the Frog.

At first glance, the newcomer seemed bent on justifying all those who characterized him as a hopeless wombat. He shouldered his burden of five sections of French courses and was seldom seen outside the Humanities Building. In fact, seldom outside his office. Actually, there were very few people who had seen the inside of his office, either. The campus community would learn much later that he had made a secret covenant with each class to meet but once a week for conversation, on condition that everyone be guaranteed a B. If they preferred an A, they had to complete of a twenty page paper on a topic of their own choice.

One of the few places that the French teacher seemed to surface was on the road by the Ozone Intercontinental Golf Links on Saturday morning, which got the athletic rumor mills going again. The OIGL was another of Palindrome's flashes of inspiration. Five years ago, the heaters and pumps at the old campus pool had finally given up the ghost, and the Gulf Cloud Athletic Conference had threatened to eject the Snarling Peccaries if they didn't come up with another sport to replace swimming. The President had the Big Idea of carving a golf course out of a reedy, undeveloped part of campus that bordered the Bullsnake River. It kept Ozone in the conference, but despite the mailing of hundreds of color brochures to other universities, athletic organizations, and church groups nation wide, no one had taken up the invitation to hold their prestige golf tournament at The Campus Where the Pines Meet the Swamps. A single yearly contest against Pittsville Tech and Golden Prairie State A and M was the only action seen on those damp fairways.

Now it appeared that Lewie the Frog must certainly be an avid golfer who had got hold of one of the brochures and realized a top quality international facility when he saw one. People expected him to go public any day in October and to announce his coup. But as October plodded along in the hot aftermath of summer, no news was forthcoming from Lewie. So Prawn Webber, a true campus leader, decided to look into the matter.

Prawn was one of Palindrome's Big Idea Men, a brain trust that hung out mostly at the campus barber shop and campus intramurals. Prawn had once been a Professor of Speech, but the low level of demand for his teaching expertise had been remedied by an administrative appointment.

It quickly became apparent from Prawn's snooping that no one had seen Lewie actually on the Ozone Intercontinental Golf Links. Further discreet probing revealed that he had never rented clubs or paid any fees at all, never even used the driving range.

The next Saturday, Prawn got in his Dodge Ram pickup and discreetly trailed Lewie as he walked from his apartment next to campus down towards the OIGL and right past it. He strolled into the main post office in town, where he must have rented a box. Then, loaded with mail, he proceeded into a run-down bar next door. Lewie was spending the better part of each Saturday morning slouched in a booth at the Patriot Lounge, polishing off a six-pack of Lone Star Beer and reading a week's worth of French newspapers. He was no golfer.

It was not until January that Prawn discovered how Lewie the Frog was spending the rest of his time. Shortly after the beginning of spring semester, an unusually thick Semester Activity Report arrived in President Palindrome's office. In principle, and according to a strict state law, every professor had to file one of these "publish or perish" updates every six months to prove his worthiness to hold an appointment at a high class institution like Ozone. But in fact, the arrival of an SAR was a rare event. For one thing, most of the Ozone faculty couldn't publish much of anything, even if the alternative was to perish. Rep. Huff McFard had solved this embarrassing problem by amending that arbitrary statute to stipulate that a report only had to be filed if a person had managed to come up with something new. "That way," Huff assured his somnolent colleagues in the legislature, "Our State Department of Education won't be bogged down reading the same old stuff about bugs and molecules, over and over." Thanks to

Huff's intervention, only a half dozen or so reports crossed the President's desk in the course of a year, listing an article in *Ozone County Genealogical Studies*, *Gulf Angler*, or *Saturday Book Reviews*. Mainly, the SAR's were used as a pretext for firing anyone who challenged the administration. "**Failure to file regular Semester Activity Reports**," the dismissal letter would read. But here was an SAR listing no fewer than seventeen publications in the space of one semester! They were all in journals with names like *Ontologica*, *Zeitschrift für gesellschaftliche Denkformen*, *Sub/Version*, *Acta Sociologica Helveticae*, and *Profondeurs*. They were all in some foreign language that President Palindrome assumed must be French, because he couldn't make heads or tails of it.

It was, appropriately, the Big Idea Man, Prawn, who first saw the golden promise of Lewie's publications. The Board of Overseers had been hassling Palindrome for years about the low productivity of most of the departments on his campus. Prawn reasoned that if they could transfer the Frog from one department to another, they could realize overnight boosts in the rate of publication. That would be all Ozone State needed to qualify for extra research money that could be used for what the

President had always wanted, a genuine slush fund.

Bursting with joy, Prawn communicated his master plan to Palindrome in the secrecy of the presidential office, but although Palindrome slapped him on the back, gave him a Garcia y Vega cigar, and promised him that Big Things would come his way, the Idea Man learned next week that his emoluments were limited to a $100.00 raise for the year and a parking space two cars closer to the exit gates for all home football games held in Peccary Stadium.

Starting immediately, Louis was rotated into a different academic department every two weeks. His entire publication record was added to the departmental output, but it was never subtracted when he moved on. This made it appear on paper that the university was undergoing a scholarly revolution of unparalleled proportions. In his next commencement address, Palindrome planned to assure the citizens of Ozone that their campus would soon be "the Stanford of the coastal plain, the Harvard of the Gulf."

It occurred to the President that he ought to get to know this Frenchman better. After all, the unique subject of conversation at the campus barber shop had shifted from the future of the baseball coach to Lewie the Frog and his prodigious scholarship.

"Just what the heeyell does that feller think he's doin' here?" everyone would ask Aldo Cappellini, the university barber.

"He's nothin' but a upstart," Aldo would sagely respond. Lewie was thus classed with an illustrious line of upstarts cited by Aldo, which went all the way through the Roosevelt administration to Al Smith and included Mahatma Gandhi, Harry Truman, Milton Berle, Adlai Stevenson, Jimmy Carter, Peewee Herman, and everyone named Kennedy.

"But there's one thing for sure," opined Prawn Webber from one of the waiting chairs. "If that Frog leaves, we're in for a rough time."

He was right. Indeed, if Lewie left at the end of the year, the Renaissance would be over for Ozone and the slush fund would evaporate as fast as real slush in the wastes of West Texas. Martin Palindrome abruptly decided that all steps must be taken to insure that Lewie did not return to the "Sourbone School" in May. So, towards the end of the spring term, the president invited his star researcher to a gala dinner in his honor at the President's House in the center of campus. The guest list read like a Who's Who of Ozone dignitaries. First, of course, was the venerable Vice President for

Student Business, Dr. Sidney Dawlfry Bolt. He was a bloated man who always looked so shiny that you suspected he had been run through one of those laminating machines that cover drivers' licenses with clear plastic. He always pretended to be deaf, mainly so that he could pretend not to hear when people deliberately or accidentally transposed his name into Dr. Sidney Ballfree Dolt. Even Mrs. Amanda Bolt was known to get a chuckle over this play on words once in a while, but tonight she was playing the obedient wifelette. Then there was Prawn Webber, in his capacity as head of the Development Council and Fighting Peccaries Booster Club, and Mrs. Prawn; Abednigo Fahrenkopf, Adjunct Assistant Vice President for Student Life, and his wife Chiquita; and Patsy Fisk (Patsy, in the History Department, had once written some speeches for a former governor and was still basking in that lukewarm glory). Finally, as a mark of distinct preference, there was Palindromes' own daughter Deewanna, called back from her condo in Fort Walton Beach specially for the occasion.

"Now, daddy, I warn you," she had pouted. "I'm not gonna do for him like I did for that contractor you had down here last year. All those games he wanted to play were just too kinky!"

"I jus' want you to be nice to this professor, that's all. What could be wrong with that? Jus' some nice conversation, and make sure he don't want to leave campus any time soon. Besides, I don't think he's . . . like the contractor. Kind of a wimp in fact. I jus' hope you can manage to get him stirred up a little bit."

"Only if you get me a new Corvette, daddy, that's my final bottom line." She had intended no pun, of course.

Palindrome okayed the car with a knowing nod. It was just a drop in the bucket compared to the slush fund he could set up if Lewie the Frog stuck around for another year or two.

As Lewie's date, Deewanna was seated right next to him. She sat there picking at her food and smiling at him, thinking of candy apple red fenders.

Across the table, Prawn had put down a barbecued chicken wing and begun to talk to Sidney Dawlfrey Bolt about his favorite topic, shrimping in the university's Tupelo Cove Biological Reserve.

"Ain't nobody gonna get nothin out of that big lake except if I want them to," he boasted. "Look, I sunk junk cars in every possible channel. Somebody no sooner puts down their nets than they snag on those wrecks. But, now, when I get ready to catch some shrimp, I jus' put down one of them old WWII tarpaulins we ordered, right over the wreck, the net passes right over the top easy as pie, and when I'm done, I got a special line rigged to pull it up again. Learned it from an old movie about submarines in WWII. How do you think I got those shrimp for this gumbo, Martin? Why, it's a bad year if I don't haul out half a ton."

"Now how's that for enterprise, Lewie?" said Palindrome, turning to the guest of honor, who had removed his loafers and was playing footsie with Deewanna under the table.

"I was under the impression, Mr. President," calmly returned de Montalte-Königbourg, "That the lake was to be maintained in a savage condition for the benefits of the marine research."

"Aw, come on, man, if I didn't drag that lake those shrimps would jus' die in there and be no good to anybody," objected Prawn, "It's six of one and half a dozen of the other."

"Indeed, I see your point."

"How about that daughter of ours," said Palindrome with a wink. "Don't you think she's about the prettiest thing in Ozone? You know she came all the way back from Florida jus' to meet you. Mother and I just insisted that she do it and we didn't even have to call her twice."

"I am sincerely glad you did not, sir, and I intend to make the most of it. It reminds me of a passage from your Shakespeare's *Troilus and Cressida* . . ."

"Dear Lewie," chortled Mrs. Palindrome, "There's no need to prove to us that you know our language. You speak much better than that Yankee we once had down from the University of . . . What was it Pa?"

"Cornell," snorted Sidney Dawlfry Bolt. "I remember that trouble¬maker came from Cornell and went straight back up there, too."

"We had him over to our house and he refused to eat my daddy's country sausage," said Mrs. Prawn petulantly. "Tried to give me some excuse about a pig's feet. It was just as rude as rude could be, and Prawn was in a mood to punch him in the mouth, weren't you dear?"

"Damn right!"

"Let's not dredge up such unpleasant subjects," said Chiquita Fahrenkopf, and turning to the guest of honor, she asked with a flutter of eyelashes, "Is it true you live in a real castle in Paris, Mr. Lewie?"

"In fact, Madame," he responded, "I merely have a modest apartment above a bakery in Neuilly. You see, I love the smell of fresh bread and . . ." But Chiquita's attention had wandered as soon as she knew Lewie did not have a real castle in Paris. She and Patsy and Lily Otto and Amanda Bolt and Mrs. Prawn were soon chatting about recipes for mayhaw jam. Meanwhile Prawn held forth on the correct procedure for catching catfish using globs of dogfood for bait. Lewie touched Deewanna's knee under the tablecloth and whispered something in her ear that made her giggle surreptitiously.

  Before long it was time for the Penguins to serve bananas Foster and coffee. The Penguins, so christened by Lily Otto, were really the black employees from Food Services dressed up in tuxedo-looking formal uniforms that were only used at the President's House. Lily had visited Charleston and Colonial Williamsburg in the company of her husband on conference trips; they skipped those boring speeches and went sightseeing. She had seen how black folks in olden times could be dressed in really cute outfits to give a lot of class to the place. When she returned to Ozone she had ordered the uniforms made up immediately at Maude's Dress Shop and Maude had outdone herself. It was true that the Food Services workers had adamantly refused to wear them until they were given that raise that Palindrome had talked about for the past ten years. And even then, they had absolutely drawn the line and refused the little powdered wigs she had purchased from the Costume Catalogue. Undeterred, Lily had stored the wigs away in hopes of a another Depression, like the one she had heard about, when the working classes could be coerced into wearing almost anything rather than take a salary cut.

      As the women were gathering to leave the men to their cigars and retire to the parlor where their raunchy conversation would not shock the delicate males too much, they could not find Deewanna. Roused from their post-prandial stupor, the men could not manage to locate Lewie, either. It was quietly assumed by both groups that The Lure had indeed achieved the desired result and "stirred him up." Thus, the evening was deemed a success.

      During the long, hot summer months, Deewanna's new red Corvette was seen almost continually parked in front of Lewie's apartment building. Her assiduousness began to provoke some surprise among Ozonians, since it was widely known that no man had been able to keep Deewanna's attention for very long. She was said to suffer from some kind of Orgasmic Deficit Disorder. So imagine how tongues began to wag when she emerged from the apartment and found it harder and harder to fit behind the steering wheel of her sportster. The sky had fallen and the impossible had happened: Deewanna was pregnant. Some of the more serious Baptists in town began to take this as a genuine pre-Apocalyptic phenomenon, akin to the moon turning to blood. After all, Deewanna's reproductive system had so far proven impervious to a prolonged and systematic onslaught from our nation's lustiest collection of young servicemen passing through the Fort Walton Beach area. There was a barracks wing at the Pensacola Naval Air Station unofficially named Deewanna Hall. In Florida, it was even rumored that she had worked her way through the entire crew of the destroyer U.S.S. Florian Heath, including a contingent of sailors previously sworn to be gay. What did Lewie have that all those boys lacked?

    Deewanna explained his appeal to her mother. "Mama, that Lewie has some imagination, all right. Better than that old lady on the sex show from Canada. Those boys in Florida would talk mighty big, but if it wasn't doggy or half-and-half, they hadn't heard of it. Not to mention all the times they were too liquored up to hold a bat. Now Lewie thinks up the most interesting things. There's this one bit he calls in French a "cooeeside royale" that just drives me wild..." Lily Otto evinced a great interest in this aspect of international linguistics, which seemed to open up a whole new area so far unexplored by her husband, despite his frequent forays to the other side of the Ozone railroad tracks.

  But far from being concerned for Deewanna's situation, her father reposed in blissful indifference. After all, the slush fund was rounding out even more quickly than Deewanna's figure. He ordered new furniture for his office, then for the President's House, then for his fishing camp, then for his beachfront condo. One day the Mercury Marquis disappeared from the presidential parking spot and was replaced by a stretch limousine ordered all the way from New Orleans and decorated with a particularly bold Snarling Peccary logo. He began organizing a grand inspection tour of some of the finest institutions of higher education in the Bahamas, the Cayman Islands, and Jamaica. The bounty of the earth was flowing his way and the intrusive lens of public scrutiny was far away, thanks to Lewie's burgeoning research. The French professor had announced that he would be back for the fall.

Meanwhile, back in Paris, Bill Hawkins posed absolutely no objection to continuing the exchange. He had taken to smoking Gauloise Caporal cigarettes, wearing black turtlenecks, and dating models from some of the minor fashion houses. His French colleagues did not object either, since his tales of Ozone life were fueling at least three doctoral dissertations on "Anglo-Saxon" social practices.

One day Louis de Montalte-Königsbourg came to visit Martin Otto at the President's Office in Jeff Davis Hall. Martin was effusive. "Lewie my boy, I couldn't be happier that you chose to stay with us. Is everything here to your satisfaction?"

"Well, in fact, sir, that is what I have come to discuss with you. I have had a most attractive offer from Golden Prairie State A and M."

Palindrome almost swallowed his cigar. After he recovered his breath, he stammered, "But, but, Looie, you can't think of that. Of course, we'll match whatever they offer. In fact, we'll top whatever they offer."

"You understand, sir, the costs of fatherhood are quite high. There is the crib, the layette, and I will need a larger place, of course…"

"I'll top whatever they offer and add five percent."

"And my little car is hardly big enough to hold an infant seat."

"There are fringes, too. I'll double your free life insurance and pick up all of your contribution to the retirement fund."

"In addition, there is the child's education to see to. My child cannot be expected to go to that place you call the Ozone Lab School. I have talked to the rector at Our Lady of Bon Secours, but their tuition is ridiculously high."

"Perhaps we could speed up your next sabbatical leave?"

"I was thinking, sir. Mr. Sidney Ballfree Dolt – pardon, Bolt – is looking quite overwhelmed these days. Perhaps it would be better, instead, to give him a little vacation? I would be happy to do what I can to see to the duties of Vice-President, strictly on a temporary basis, of course..."

Martin Palindrome didn't know what to say. This seemed to be something like what he had heard called an altimutum, or something like that. De Montalte could practically hear the unoiled gears churning away in the presidential skull. Sid Bolt had his own friends and relatives in the legislature and he would put up a monumental fight rather than be passed over at his age. Could Martin count on Rep. Huff McFard, who had been absent in Vegas through most of the past two legislative sessions, to muster forces that would protect his presidency? Suddenly he realized he was in too deep and had no choice. He pushed the buzzer to summon his secretary.

"Miss Doozer, Vice-President Bolt needs to take some time off. Draw up a list of likely replacements. Start with the French faculty."

"It looks like I should go shopping for a new automobile."

"It wouldn't be fit for an acting Vice-President to drive around in an old, dented Honda."

De Montalte put his hand on the president's shoulder. "Martin," said Lewie. "I think this is the beginning of a beautiful friendship."

Naturally, Sidney Dawlfrey Bolt was not going to take this affront lying down. But that is another story.

Diogenes in King George County

Mel and Bill were on a two hundred acre woodlot out by Index. They had gone early to hunt for a couple of hours and set up their stands in oak trees on either side of a little ridge a hundred yards apart. Pawley had told them the deer would come up the gullies and that way if one of them spooked a group over the ridge, they might run right into the other's range of fire. But it must have been too cold or too foggy because the deer never came up either gulley.

They had just finished breaking down and packing their gear on the four wheeler when they saw a strange light shining where the deer should have been. It seemed to lurch from side to side as it got closer and they thought about grabbing their shotguns. But just then they heard a thud and a plaintive "Ow!" as the light seemed to arc straight up. Running to see what happened, they found Bobo Winters flat on his back next to a tree, rubbing his nose, still holding a flashlight in his other hand.

Mel asked, "What the hell are you doing out here, Bobo? It's hunting season and you could get yourself shot."

Bobo took a deep breath and said, "Looking for an honest man. Are you honest?" He came within whiskey sniffing distance and peered into Mel's eyes. "I don't think so. Somebody stole my truck. Did you steal it?"

"Now be reasonable, Bobo. If I had stolen your truck, would I be out here in the woods with my four-wheeler?"

"Reason's got nothin' to do with it!" Bobo turned with a jerk to Bill. "What about you, did you steal it?"

"No, sir, I didn't either."

"One of you is lyin' and I can tell which one. If a liar says he did something then the opposite is true and he didn't do it. Ha! Gotcha!"

"That's just what we said," said Bill, "We didn't do it. Q. E. D."

Bobo looked confused and then frowned, "People is trash."

"Why don't you just tell us what happened?" suggested Bill.

"It all started at Mulkey's. We was havin' a drink and playin' some Omaha poker and finally I won so much the game broke up and Mulkey closed and everybody headed home. I looked for the keys to my truck and then I couldn't find my wad of bills and I realized, 'My God, somebody robbed me of my winnin's!"

"Are you sure you didn't leave them at the bar?" ventured Mel.

"If I had left them there, why would I have my keys? Huh? Anyway, I drove out the county road to where it bends and I felt the call of nature, so I stopped for the pause that refreshes. And I brought this here flashlight when I went into the brush so I wouldn't trip over nothin'. Well, after I was refreshed, I was straightenin' up and I felt this pint of Jack Daniels in my pocket, so I thought, 'Why not?' and I sat down on a fallen log and had me a few sips. And after a while, I went on back to the road and my truck was gone, 'cause some dishonest bastard had stole it right after some other dishonest bastard, or maybe even the same one, had stole my wad of cash. That's why I say there's no more honest men around here no more."

"When was that?" asked Mel. "Mulkey usually closes at 2:30."

"Damn straight! I must have been stumblin' around in this forest for hours lookin' for those varmints."

"Why didn't you just follow the county road, or if you were going to cut through the woods, just walk in a straight line. Sooner or later you would have to come out somewhere instead of going in circles forever. Probably you just came out around the bend from your truck and couldn't see it. It simply appeared to be stolen."

"It didn't appear at all, it disappeared, that's what I'm telling you. Nobody cares about nothin' any more. I might never have come out of the trees and wound up dying of hydrodermia and nobody would know until they found my skeleton . Serves 'em right for stealin' my truck and my money and everything."

"Seems to me," observed Bill, "that you would be on the losing end of that score. Hell, you didn't know where you were or which way you were headed and you barely had any idea who you were."

"I know who I am. I remember it from high school." He seemed to visualize a long-forgotten book. "Unaccommodated man, that's what they call it."

"Okay, well for now, Mr. Unaccommodated, we better see about getting you back to your own accommodations. Hop up on the back of the four wheeler and we'll take you back to the county road."

Bobo tried to settle himself on the back of the vehicle and promptly slid off. Mel got up from the passenger side. "Here, you better sit up here or you'll drop off and break your neck. I'll ride in back."

Bobo grinned and pulled the pint from his pocket as he sat down. "You're a true man after all. Have a swig as your reward."

Mel chuckled and gestured no. "I guess you believe in Mulkey's motto: in vino veritas."

"I ain't no wino!" Bobo protested, "I only drink Miller's and Jack Daniels. Quit casting your 'spersions on me."

"Bobo, if I wasn't myself and could be anybody else, I sure wouldn't want to be you."

The Witches of Okemos

Christmas was coming and somewhere the geese were getting fat, but the same could not be said of my wallet. I could certainly not afford to ante up the $200.00 for even the most reduced airline ticket from East Lansing, Michigan back home to Boston. True, I could just barely afford a bus or train, but I rejected both as offering nothing at all that was new. I'd seen the extremes humanity could go to in order to survive life within New York's train terminals and I'd experienced the dirty void of the Pittsburgh Greyhound station through the middle of the night. I figured it was time to consult the ride board at the Student Union. One notice caught my eye: it was seeking a male passenger to Boston on just the right day for a mere $25 share of the gas. I called and informed a demure female who answered that I was interested in the ride offer if it was still available. She replied that indeed, it was, but I would have to present myself at an address in neighboring Okemos to "talk things over." This made me fear some snobbish rejection might be in store, but the street was just over the border from East Lansing, well within walking distance, so I strolled over there.

It was a modest little one-story house built back in the forties. Perhaps she might not be so snobbish after all. I rang the bell and it was answered by a face that matched the voice on the phone: regular but unremarkable, equally devoid of makeup and enthusiasm, crowned by straight, somewhat mousy hair draped atop a spindly frame. She introduced herself as Carol, shook hands with me limply and somewhat reluctantly and led me in to meet Laura, who turned out to be almost a carbon copy of Carol, but a bit shorter and a shade or two closer to blonde.

"We apologize for making you come," began Carol. "But we felt we really wanted to be able to ride with somebody we trust, because of all the weirdoes who seem to be around these days."

My ample beard and purple beads apparently didn't automatically qualify me as a weirdo, so they were probably not hippie-haters, but the lack of any offer of liquid refreshment made me wary they might be some kind of austere fundamentalists, especially in light of their grayish attire and the neutral apartment décor.

"I don't blame you at all. I wouldn't like to ride with a weirdo either."

"You seem honest," observed Laura. "Can you do some driving and do you have the $25 in cash?"

"Right here," I said, taking two sawbucks and a five out of my wallet as though they had a lot of company. "And I'm willing to pay it up front, too. As for driving, no problem, stick or automatic."

"The money can wait till later, but we have to be careful all parties are comfortable with this arrangement," explained Carol.

"Is there anyone else who is coming besides you two?"

"Actually, we were thinking about you."

"Excuse me, but neither of you seems too intimidating. Do you have some kind of contagious disease I should know about?"

"Of course not," giggled Laura. "I meant that you shouldn't have any worries about our beliefs."

"A chacun son goût," I quipped. When they both donned quizzical expressions, I continued, "Sorry, I'm a French major. Everyone has a right to their own tastes."

"Yes, but are you really SINCERE about that?" said Carol.

"As far as I know."

"Sometimes people pretend to be sincere, or think they actually are sincere, and then they find that something bothers them when they find out all about it."

"Why not try me? I'm a big boy and I don't think I'll be too shocked by anything."

"Alright, well, I guess we can check...," hesitated Carol, as she looked to Laura for a nod.

Then she looked me straight in the eyes. "We're Wiccan."

At first I thought they were simply using a bit of Boston dialect. "Wicked what?"

"No, Wiccan. We are witches."

She had clearly said witches. Perhaps she was referring to her town.

"Are you from Salem?" Our Naugatuck Bulldogs regularly tackled with the Salem Witches for the big Halloween football rivalry.

"No, we're from right here. We're Okemos witches. And we're very different from Salem witches anyway."

"Of course," I conceded. "Anyway, most of those trials were actually based on greedy real estate transactions."

"Really?" responded Carol. "I'll have to read up on that."

"Try *The Devil in Massachusetts.*"

"Anyway, do you know anything about white witchcraft? Could it be you might be a believer, too?"

"I'm afraid not. My family is more into Odin." It was true that three-quarters of my ancestors once yearned for the afterlife in Valhalla.

"Odin, Lord of the Hanged?" inquired Laura with a hint of interest.

"That's a bit grim," I said. "I prefer to think of him as Odin, Lord of Battles, Keeper of All Oaths, Possessor of Runic Knowledge, Ruler of the Eternal Hall of Heroes."

They stared at me with slightly open mouths. Perhaps I should have admitted that I was currently a Unitarian, but they might have mocked me with the usual rejoinder that I simply couldn't decide what to believe in.

However, after a pause, they both nodded and said, "I think we'll get along very well." Clearly, they had classified me as a fellow-traveler, in all senses of the word.

I came back two days later at the appointed departure time and slung my duffel bag down by their plain blue van.

"Is that all you have?" a surprised Laura asked.

"I like to travel light and eat heavy."

"Well, if you don't mind, could you help us with some of our things?"

She showed me into a room where they had prepared their paraphernalia, obviously much more massive than mine. I took what appeared to be the heaviest box. Meanwhile, the two girls seemed to content to putter around, wrapping up various objects carefully in crepe paper. When I came back, they pointed to an open box they had placed by the door. I looked in. It was filled with big, expensive-looking candles.

"How come these are black?"

"Oh, they're for the Black Mass, of course."

"Sure."

There were also some big candelabras, a crystal skull, and various other genuine witch regalia. I felt perhaps I should have packed more: maybe a long wooden staff or some mystical stones, or at least a big floppy hat, just to place poor Odin on an equal plane.

Laura drove first, meticulously observing every traffic law to the letter and never even approaching the speed limit, the only Michigander I have ever seen behave in that fashion, before or since. When muscle cars sped past, she would admonish them, "You'll just have to slow down sooner or later!" If someone flipped her the finger for "holding up traffic," the worst she would mutter was "Oh, piff, what a sorehead."

Somewhere near that Metropolis of Sin, London, Ontario, she announced she was getting tired and went back to take a snooze in the van, while Carol took my place in the shotgun seat and I got behind the wheel. I asked her their destination, not being able to get Salem out of my mind.

"We're heading out to Provincetown eventually to meet with a coven, but we're staying at my sister's place in Revere overnight. Is that close enough for you?'

"Perfect. I can practically walk home if necessary."

"So, with that Odin thing," she began, squirming a bit. "Do you have to do any blood-letting or sacrifice or anything?"

"Not that I'm aware of. I thought that was more in your line isn't it?"

"Oh, no. Not with white magic. If we need to use blood, we just get some from a meat market. They usually don't ask any questions at all. Who knows? Maybe lots of people are collecting blood for all kinds of reasons. Personally, I couldn't stand chopping off chicken heads the way those Santeria people do. But I've read about the Vikings and that "Blood Eagle" execution they used."

"Well, if I ever defeat a really nasty enemy that I'm really mad at, maybe I'll consider cutting his ribs away from his backbone, prying them open, and tearing out his beating heart, but so far I've never been in a situation where that seemed appropriate."

"You wouldn't eat it, would you?" she asked, as she blanched.

"Of course not! Who knows what that kind of person had been up to? I suppose the proper thing to do would be to stick it up on a pole for birds of prey. Odin is particularly close to eagles and crows."

"I bet you wouldn't even be afraid to go to one of those Santeria things," she sighed, somewhat enviously.

"Por que no, chiquita? Salud a todos los poderosos!"

But her Spanish was no better than her French.

After a few hours and various remarks about the weather and the grunginess of the Buffalo area, we were greeted by Laura, refreshed by her nap. She offered each of us an oatmeal bar and then whispered to Carol, "You should come back here so we can try on the clothes."

They disappeared behind the curtain that separated the back of the van from the driver's compartment. After a while, I heard some squeals of delight, then a bit more whispering. Finally Laura stuck her head through the curtain and announced, "We've changed into some different clothes. You wouldn't be offended if we showed them to you, would you?'

"Absolutely not!" I responded, hoping vaguely for some kind of black leather witches' bikinis.

They drew back the curtain to reveal that they were both clad in the uniforms of altar boys.

"It's for the ritual. We wanted something new to look our very best. What do you think?"

Well, I was obviously a bit disappointed about the lack of erotic lingerie, and I was still pretty stupid about the opposite sex, but I had learned enough about women to know there is only one possible answer to that kind of question. Gulping back any negative thoughts and assuming a glowing countenance, I enthused, "They're just right! They're really becoming on you. And they make you look very... seriously... Wiccan!"

"Oh, good!" Carol actually clapped her hands. "You're not bothered by the cross-dressing thing, then?'

"Well, I never found anything in the petite section that would suit me, but you two look really great in those." I decided not to add that during my Catholic childhood I had always thought those little lacy frocks looked a little unsuitable on boys, especially my old friend Mike, who had also played third base on the local team.

I decided to inquire further into sartorial matters. "Do your male counterparts, warlocks or whatever you call them, wear girl's clothes?"

"Well," thought Laura, "They do wear robes, if you call that girl's clothes, but we usually don't think of them that way."

Carol suppressed a little laugh and confided, "Sometimes we can get naked and change around. That's what I really like."

"I'm sure that's what I would prefer, too."

"But of course, you couldn't participate in a ritual."

"Why not, don't you proselytize?"

"Not really. And besides, it wouldn't be appropriate to share loyalties to Our Powers with someone like Odin," opined Carol.

"Not that we deny his existence or anything!" disclaimed Laura. "That would be completely at odds with the beliefs of witchcraft!" She looked a bit afraid, as though I might rat out the entire Wiccan conspiracy to the Norse pantheon. Perhaps she was picturing Odin as Godfather, sending his hit man Thor with orders to squash all witches under the marvelous hammer, Mjollnir.

She continued, "It's just that our order is very clear about matters of loyalty. We have our standards and I imagine you have yours. You would never consider giving them up, would you?"

"No way!" I affirmed. "No straw death on a mattress for me, no underworld beneath a moldering, smelly barrow. I'll die with a weapon in my hand and a war cry on lips and I'll already be able to taste that roast boar and mead waiting for me up there in the clouds at the end of the rainbow bridge, where the Valkyrie will guide me and Good Heimdall will hail my arrival."

They both smiled, but later I heard Carol mutter into Laura's ear, "How unearthly!"

After Carol did her stint at the wheel along the Mass Turnpike, with me at shotgun again (for neither of them had even made the slightest hint of seducing me to the loyalty to Their Powers), we motored into spaghetti-rich Revere and were greeted by the sister and her brood, who had counted on the witches' punctuality and were on the sidewalk awaiting us. I reached for my duffle, but Laura and Carol insisted on lighting a couple of the black candles, since I had been such a good and financially reliable companion, and pronouncing over me a little litany of words that sounded like Tolkien had invented them for dwarves or elves. I thanked them and headed down the street for the Blue Line to Wonderland, where I could relay to a bus for Lynn and Naugatuck. I did not feel the least bit diabolical for my experience with Satan's brides.

ABOUT THE AUTHOR

After a forty year career teaching language and literature, James F. Gaines has concentrated on his own poetry and fiction, as well as working with the writing community in Fredericksburg, Virginia. He collaborates with his son John Manley Roberts Gaines to create the science fiction universe of the Forlani Saga novels, including *Life Sentence, Spy Station* and *Earth Regained*.

Made in the USA
Columbia, SC
05 March 2018